S0-BVX-853

"Marilee," Cole … ***golden girl. You h***… ***With your beautiful red hair you're like a goddess, so lovely, so desirable."***

"Pure nonsense. You're ridiculous. I'm a plain, ordinary school teacher," she whispered, but his words worked their seduction.

He kissed her throat and said, "Honey, you're more tempting than any woman I've ever met." His blue eyes held her spellbound while he whispered, "This is destiny, it's got to be. I'm never here this time of year. And how often have you crashed a balloon?"

His mouth conquered her protests, made her senses clamor for more. Ablaze, she returned his kisses with unbridled eagerness, her tongue meeting his. Hot, intimate, each clash sent wild tingles racing.

Her response was primordial, timeless. Her need mushroomed, spreading its fury, compelling her to yield.

Marilee groaned in anguish. "Stop, Cole! We can't be feeling this!"

"Of course not," he breathed. But like candlelight in a blizzard her protests were futile. She swayed as he held her, his dark hands caressing her pale skin.

"You know this is special," Cole said, the words coming from deep in his throat, ground out in a breathlessness that made her feel as if she were the only woman in the world for him.

"Cole, please," Marilee answered, "we hardly know each other."

His arms tightened around her. "You're going to know me better than you've ever known anyone on earth."

WHAT ARE *LOVESWEPT* ROMANCES?

They are stories of true romance and touching emotion. We believe those two very important ingredients are constants in our highly sensual and very believable stories in the *LOVESWEPT* line. Our goal is to give you, the reader, stories of consistently high quality that may sometimes make you laugh, sometimes make you cry, but are always fresh and creative and contain many delightful surprises within their pages.

Most romance fans read an enormous number of books. Those they truly love, they keep. Others may be traded with friends and soon forgotten. We hope that each *LOVESWEPT* romance will be a treasure—a "keeper." We will always try to publish

LOVE STORIES YOU'LL NEVER FORGET
BY AUTHORS YOU'LL ALWAYS REMEMBER

The Editors

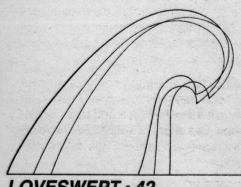

LOVESWEPT • 42

Sara Orwig
Heat Wave

 BANTAM BOOKS • TORONTO • NEW YORK • LONDON • SYDNEY

HEAT WAVE
A Bantam Book / April 1984

*LOVESWEPT and the wave device are trademarks of
Bantam Books, Inc.*

All rights reserved.
Copyright © 1984 by Sara Orwig.
Cover art copyright © 1984 by Max Ginsburg.
*This book may not be reproduced in whole or in part, by
mimeograph or any other means, without permission.
For information address: Bantam Books, Inc.*

ISBN 0-553-21655-4

Published simultaneously in the United States and Canada

Bantam Books are published by Bantam Books, Inc. Its
trademark, consisting of the words ''Bantam Books'' and the
portrayal of a rooster, is Registered in U.S. Patent and Trademark Office and in other countries. Marca Registrada. Bantam
Books, Inc., 666 Fifth Avenue, New York, New York 10103.

PRINTED IN THE UNITED STATES OF AMERICA

O   0 9 8 7 6 5 4 3 2 1

One

As the bright yellow hot-air balloon gained speed in its descent to the ground, Marilee O'Neil worked frantically to keep it aloft. She looked below. Sprawled on the ground, like an oasis in a desert, was a house, barns, and sheds surrounded by miles of shimmering golden Kansas wheat. Behind the green-roofed house the clear aqua water of a swimming pool sparkled. A man was stretched on a chaise, but he sat up, shading his eyes, as the balloon neared his pool.

Marilee's heart thudded in fright as the big balloon's wobbly, angled descent brought her closer and closer to the blue-green water of the swimming pool. She desperately fiddled with the manual controls. If only she could hit the pool and not the house or concrete or trees! The sunbather jumped to his feet.

Abandoning the controls, Marilee didn't know whether to scream or close her eyes. Instead, frozen in terror, she clung to the wicker gondola. As it bore down, she thought she would drop right on top of the man.

"Look out!" she yelled.

The balloon plunged faster. She was close enough to see every detail below her. The man stood at the edge of the pool, watching her approach. For an instant she was sufficiently startled to forget her predicament. He was nude, deeply tanned, and very fit. He was standing with his fingers splayed on his bare hips. That strip of flesh was pale, contrasting with the rest of his tanned body. On his chest, below broad, muscular shoulders, a mat of curly dark hair tapered to a narrow line across the hard planes of his flat stomach.

A high stake fence surrounded the pool area. Inside the fence were flowerbeds, trees, bright blue wrought-iron pool furniture that matched the large umbrella over a round table. Surrounding the out-side were elm trees. The balloon swept over their tops, and Marilee saw the concrete looming up, then the pool. Screaming, she clutched the edge of the gondola as it crashed into the water.

She lost her balance and fell, then tumbled out, and cold water swamped her. Gasping, she surfaced, shook her red hair out of her eyes, and treaded water. The man stood at the edge of the pool with his arms folded over his chest. He seemed oblivious to his nudity.

"At least wrap a towel around yourself!" she shouted.

He threw back his head and laughed. She didn't want to climb out and talk to a naked man. She stared off to the side at a tall native elm a few yards beyond the pool. "That wasn't meant to be funny."

"I have a ten-foot fence," he said, "armed guards, an alarm system to insure my privacy. You manage to surmount all obstacles, invade my privacy, ruin my peace, and then have the nerve to tell me to get dressed!"

Making an effort not to lower her gaze from his face, to try to forget the blatant masculinity that pulled at her like a magnet, she stared at his eyes. They were startlingly blue. "I'm sorry if I invaded your privacy, but I couldn't control the balloon."

"Maybe you shouldn't have been up there flying it."

"I have a license. I've had fourteen hours of flight time. If you'll do the gentlemanly thing and wrap a towel around your middle, I'll get out of your pool and your life."

"And if I don't do the gentlemanly thing?" he asked, laughter filling every word.

Anger was now added to her embarrassment. "I would have the rotten luck to drop into a pool owned by a . . ."

"A what?"

"An exhibitionist!"

Another laugh burst from him, making her angrier as her attention returned to the elm. "I didn't say that to amuse you either. You *are* an exhibitionist."

"Like hell, lady. I was minding my own business in my own pool on my own property when you descended."

She clamped her lips together, risking another look at his blue eyes. They were filled with a devilish twinkle. "May I use your phone?" she asked.

"Are you married?"

"What does that have to do with your phone?"

"I'll bet you're not."

"Why do you think I'm single?"

"If you were married I don't think you'd have such a hang-up about a nude male body."

"I don't have a hang-up about naked males."

"Hah! *Are* you married?"

"No. Now may I use your phone?"

"Who are you?"

"You know, you're really aggravating."

She couldn't help another peek at his laughing blue eyes. His grin was very appealing. Brown locks of hair curled over his forehead and his firm jaw and prominent cheekbones made his features rugged. His smile was irresistible. Almost irresistible. She wanted to get away from him. He was beginning to make her very nervous. She shifted her gaze back to the elm. "I don't want to remain in your pool all day."

"Get out."

"Where's the phone?"

"Will you have dinner with me?"

"You've got to be kidding!"

"Nope. You dropped in, you might as well stay for dinner."

"Thank you, no."

"That's a disappointment. How'd you get way out here anyway?"

Remembering the frantic past hour, she bit her lip. "That's a long story. To make it short, I have a friend who was supposed to race his balloon. When he broke his arm, I said I'd fly in his place."

"Looks like you lost the race. You're not married, but there's a man in your life."

"You might say so, yes. Are you going to let me use the phone?"

"Are you engaged?"

"No. You ask terribly personal questions. It's just my luck to fall into the swimming pool of some perverted male. May I use your phone?"

"After you agree to have dinner with me."

"Thanks, but I have to get back to town." Silence descended. Smelling of chlorine, the pool water lapped gently around her while she studied the elm, its broad green leaves, its spreading limbs. Actually, the pool was deliciously cool on this hot May day, but she wanted to go home. She couldn't tread water indefinitely, though, and she couldn't hang on to the wicker gondola for it was slowly filling with water and starting to sink. In the perimeter of her vision she could see that he wasn't moving. The silence was stretching tautly between them, grating her nerves until she felt thoroughly frustrated by the wordless contest of wills. Her gaze felt pulled as if by ropes. Finally, she looked at him again.

"I'm Cole Chandler."

"How do you do, Mr. Chandler. May I please, please use your phone?"

"Sure. After you agree to stay for dinner."

"You're really nuts!"

He chuckled. "And you are . . ."

She didn't answer. He tried again. "C'mon, honey. What's your name?"

"Don't call me honey!"

"Whooo. Another hang-up."

Without thinking, she looked at him. He was grinning, a wide, inviting grin full of mischief.

"Are you going to hold me here against my will?"

"I'm not holding you at all. Honey—"

"My name is Marilee. Don't call me honey."

"Oh? Any reason I can't call you 'honey'? Are you scared of it or has there been some 'honey' incident in your past?"

"You're really crazy! I fell into the pool of a crazy man."

He laughed, a deep-throated, full laugh that almost melted her anger.

She talked to the tree. "Look here, I need to use your phone. I want to get out of here. Everyone will be looking for me." And her arms and legs were getting tired.

"Everyone? You must be very, very popular, Marilee . . . Marilee . . . ?"

"Marilee O'Neil and don't be ridiculous. The chase vehicle lost sight of me and my friend will be looking for me. He'll be worried."

"Ahh, him again. How important is he to you?"

"That's none of your business. I'm getting tired of staring at your elm tree while I tread water. Will you please put a towel around your middle?"

"Marilee O'Neil. Other than my name, do you know who I am?"

Her head jerked around. "How would I know who you are?"

"You're in my swimming pool. You might have wanted to meet me."

"Do people go to this length to meet you?"

"Sometimes."

She couldn't believe such a thing. He was the most aggravating male she had ever encountered in all her thirty years.

But he was appealing, without a doubt. His blue eyes were inviting, sexy. His smile was definitely irresistible, his thick brown hair an inviting tangle. That first image of a broad-shouldered, slim-hipped virile male was impossible to forget. Squelching her thoughts, she glared at him. "You're an exhibitionist, a crazy egotist!"

"Such flattery, Marilee. That sounds like a Texas name."

"No, Tennessee originally. My parents moved to Kansas from Tennessee. I'm getting tired of this."

"Well, Marilee, if you're tired, get out of the pool. Would you like something to drink?"

"You know the only thing I'd like is a telephone."

"And you know that as soon as you consent to have dinner with me, I'll get the telephone."

"I'm not a pickup!"

He laughed again. "No, you're not. You dropped in on me like a bomb."

"That isn't what I meant. I don't know you or anything about you."

"You know more about me right now than some people I've worked with for years," he drawled.

She burned with embarrassment and anger. "I had the grace not to look."

His mocking grin told her he knew better. Blushing furiously, she amended her answer. "I haven't looked since the first time. Not that it would bother you." She thought again about his questioning her if she knew who he was. "Oh, Lord, are you a model for one of those nude male magazines?"

"I look familiar?" He was definitely laughing again.

"No! You seemed to think I might recognize you. It's logical to think you might be a male model."

"Thank you. I'll trust your judgment on the matter."

"I don't know anything about the magazines."

"Oh? Then why did you think I might be pictured in them?"

"Because you have the body for it and you're oblivious to your nudity."

"I have the body for it?"

"Where is that phone?"

"What about—"

"As for tonight, I know nothing about you. The little I do know isn't reassuring."

He waved his hand. "My house ought to be reassuring."

She glanced at the sprawling two-story white frame house. "Just because you have a big home doesn't mean anything."

"It does to a lot of people. Do you work?"

"I'm a reading teacher and a painter."

"My teachers never looked like you. What kind of painter? Oils, watercolor?"

"House."

"You paint houses?"

"When I'm not teaching. It's nice work and brings in money." Why was she telling him that?

"Want to paint my house?"

Startled, she looked at the house again, then turned back to the tree. "It doesn't need it."

"Do you always turn down work so quickly?"

"No. What business are you in?"

"I'm a farmer."

She forgot the elm. "You're not!" She didn't believe him for a minute. He didn't look or act like a farmer. She'd bet he'd never seen a plow in his life. "We've had quite a chat and I'm getting tired of treading water. May I use your phone?"

"You know the condition."

Consternation shook her. She thought about her drifting flight. During the last hour she hadn't seen a house or store for miles in any direction. She needed to get back to Wichita. Water lapped gently at her neck as she kept her hands and feet moving to stay afloat. She glanced behind her. The gondola was almost completely submerged while the silky yellow envelope, the material of the balloon, hid a bed of flowers, covered patio furniture, and draped over the side of the pool into the water. She knew how much Jack must be suffering, wondering about his balloon, if not about her.

There seemed only one recourse. "Okay," she told the tree, "I'll have dinner with you if you promise—"

"Whoa! No promises."

"How do I know you're not a rapist?"

In a sexy drawl that sent a shiver racing through her, he answered, "Marilee, honey, you'll have to take my word. I'm not a rapist."

She knew he told the truth. He looked like the type of man who had spent most of his life surrounded by very willing females. It rankled though to be at his mercy. She tilted her chin higher. "I wouldn't expect you to admit it or announce the fact."

"I promise. You're safe from rape. Maybe not from seduction . . ."

Her temper matched the heat of the Kansas sunshine. "I'll be safe from that! I'll have dinner with you. In my wet shorts and halter. Now get me a phone and put a towel around you."

"You want some of my clothes? They won't fit, but they'll be dry."

"Thank you, no. I'll be happy if you'll just put on your clothes."

"I thought a towel would satisfy you."

"It will! I promised I'd stay for dinner. Where's the phone?" His laughter irritated her. "Do you think everything in life is funny?"

"Hardly, but I haven't ever met anyone like you, Marilee."

A sudden thought struck her. "Are you a nudist?"

"No."

"Are you eating dinner nude?"

"Not unless you will too."

"Indeed, I won't! You can take your telephone and—"

"Hey!"

Through clenched teeth she said, "I'm not eating in the nude."

"That's very disappointing. You can look now."

"What?"

"I'm perfectly respectable. I have a towel over the offensive region."

So he did. A white towel was secured around his narrow hips and draped at an angle across a flat stomach, barely touching his muscular tanned thighs. Why would a man with a body like a professional boxer have armed guards, an alarm system, an elegant, enormous house in the middle of nowhere? Thoughts of a gangster, the mob, suddenly came to mind.

"Where's the phone?" Swimming to the edge of the pool, she climbed out to face him. Water splashed off her, squishing out of her sneakers, leaving her yellow halter and shorts plastered to her body.

With a leisurely scrutiny, his blue gaze moved at a snail's pace over her halter, which clung to her full breasts, revealing every curve.

His voice was low, husky, and sexy. "And you were angry with me because I didn't have on any clothes!"

Fully aware she was barely clothed, that the wet halter might as well have been nonexistent, she blushed. He made her want to fling her hands in front of herself to try and hide from his devouring blue eyes. "Will you please not look at me like that!"

"Honey, there are some things a man just can't resist doing," he drawled and continued his survey, his gaze dropping down to study her long, slender legs as she slipped the uncomfortably wet sneakers off. "My, oh my, oh my! I knew when I got up this morning, today would be a good day."

Determined not to let him upset her, she raised her chin. "You're not keeping your part of the bargain."

"I didn't say a word about looking at you. The phone is right there on that table."

It was only a few feet away! Her anger rushed

back full force. "You could have handed the phone to me while I was in the water. It's cordless!"

He grinned. "That wouldn't have been any fun at all and I wouldn't have a dinner date."

"You aren't fair! To add to your list of vile characteristics, you're a cheat, Mr. Chandler."

"It achieved what I wanted."

She was certain he was a gangster. Farming! Farmers were the salt of the earth. They were pleasant, reliable, trustworthy people. And they worked hard. They didn't lie around nude, sunbathing all day.

"Where am I? I'll have to give someone directions to come pick me up."

"I'll take you home after dinner."

"Oh, no! Not on your life. Just tell me where I am."

The corners of his mouth lifted slowly. He grinned, remaining infuriatingly silent.

"You have to tell me where I am! Someone will have to come get the balloon. Or what's left of it."

"I'll take you and the remains home."

"It'll be trouble."

"No, bother, honey."

The subject was closed. A flutter of panic disturbed her and, picking up the blue phone, she punched the numbers vigorously to vent her frustration.

As the phone on the other end rang; she shook wet strands of red hair away from her face and glanced over her shoulder. Only a few feet away Cole Chandler stood with his hands on his narrow hips, blatantly eyeing her.

She turned her back to him when she heard Jack say hello.

"Jack, this is Marilee." The explosion that she had expected came. She held the receiver away from her ear, listening to his fuming and cursing. During the first quarter hour of the race, Jack had followed her and they had kept in contact by CB radio. Shortly after that, he had told her she was drifting too far off course, then they had lost contact. As he described to her his anguish of the last few hours, she could imagine his angry brown eyes, the lock of straight brown hair that fell over his forehead. When he gave her a chance to speak, she said, "I'm sorry. After I got off course, I don't know what happened."

"While you sailed off at a crazy angle, my car stalled," he said, obviously still upset. "I couldn't keep sight of you. Where are you now?"

"I don't know."

"Marilee . . ."

"Jack, I'm at a home of a man named Cole Chandler. I'm way out in nowhere. It's in the middle of a wheat field."

"I've heard of Cole Chandler. Is it a big fancy house?"

"Yes."

"Give me directions and I'll be right out to get you."

"Wait a minute, Jack. I'm staying for dinner."

"You're what?"

"He invited me for dinner."

"Marilee, you don't even know the man."

"I'm sorry, but I'm staying for dinner."

"Where's the balloon?"

She drew a long breath. How she hated to answer that question. It was worse than telling Jack she was staying for dinner. She and Jack dated occasionally but he wasn't interested beyond friendship. The balloon was different. Jack loved the balloon. How could she tell him she had just destroyed the object of his affections?

"Where's my balloon?" he repeated testily.

"I have insurance. I'll pay for it, Jack."

"Dammit, where is it?"

"In the swimming pool."

She held the receiver away from her ear while Jack swore a steady stream.

Cole stepped close enough behind her that she could feel the heat of his body. "It seems the man is more interested in his balloon than in you," he drawled. "I take it there's nothing serious between you."

"That's right." Embarrassed, she raised the receiver. "Jack, I'll pay for it. I'm sorry it happened."

"I knew it! Is the gondola in the water? My CB?"

"Yes."

"I knew you'd do this! I shouldn't have listened when you said you wanted to fly it for me. That bullheaded independence of yours has done it now!"

"If I get you another one, won't it be all right?"

Cole took the receiver out of her hand.

"This is Cole Chandler," he said in a business-like voice. "Pick out another balloon, mister, and send the bill to me. I'll buy you a new one, whatever kind and price you want. I'll keep this as a souvenir."

Marilee burned with rage. "You'll do not such thing!"

Cole calmly replaced the receiver.

"You hung up on him! I wasn't through talking and you're not buying Jack another balloon!"

The look in his eyes sent a message as clear as a telegram. He wasn't listening to a word she said.

His blue eyes devoured her, consuming every thought in her head except the realization that she suddenly felt as if she had picked up a live wire.

"Now, Marilee, I'm going to collect payment for the balloon."

Two

His voice was husky and coaxing. Its deep timbre was like a touch, sending a shiver through her. Even so, she started to answer coolly, to stop the pass that she knew was coming. But the words lodged in her throat, melting away as she met his gaze.

Their communication changed from verbal to physical and the impact was dazzling.

The depths of his blue eyes seemed deeper than his swimming pool. And it was going to be a thousand times more difficult to stay afloat. The air between them was so electric with tension, Marilee was surprised lightning didn't spark.

Suddenly Cole Chandler wasn't just a stranger, just a man. Instead he was a wonderful, exciting man. Her consciousness of him had jumped into a different realm.

She became interested in him, acutely aware of him physically beyond anything she would have believed possible. It was as if she were myopic and someone had dropped corrective lenses over her eyes. Time was suspended. The moment was prolonged and became one of monumental importance.

His chest expanded with a shuddering breath and she knew that he felt the overpowering magnetism too.

With distracting confidence, he whispered, "Come here, honey." His gaze caught her; his seductive tone reeled her in. As he put his arms around her waist to draw her near, she acquiesced languorously.

She was still wet from the pool. He was warm and dry. His rough terrycloth towel pressed against her bare skin above the waistband of her shorts. She put her hands on his chest, entranced with the crisp short brown curls as they tickled her palms, and the hard muscles beneath them.

The mere contact of her flesh on his was riveting. His skin smelled of suntan lotion. She knew better than to let him kiss her. Sure she did. So why was it so difficult to refuse?

As she started to push away, he chuckled. "If you struggle, the towel you wanted me to wear will be gone."

She froze and his arms crushed her to him. Her skimpy wet halter was little barrier between them. His thick chest hair was a sensuous treat to her wet breasts. Drowning out all sounds, her heart drummed in her ears as he leaned down.

His lips possessed hers, taking command in a hard, deliberate kiss. His tongue thrust into her mouth with an arrogant force, sending a startling shock from head to toe as it drank in her sweetness, explored her, set off a hundred tiny explosions.

Agony burst inside, radiating, filling her with

seductive torment. She dazedly wrapped her arms around him, feeling the firm muscles in his back.

He lifted his head and studied her with an expression she couldn't fathom, with blue eyes that had darkened to the color of a stormy Kansas sky.

As she slanted her gaze up beneath dark auburn lashes, she exhaled slowly. Her heavy-lidded eyes didn't want to stay open and she felt as if she were slowly being anesthetized. Every inch of her skin was sensitive, aware of the faintest brush of his male frame.

He drew a sharp breath. When he spoke, his voice was low, unsteady. "You're really something, Marilee."

"So are you." *Something I should avoid like the plague.* She was in more danger now than when she had plunged out of the sky to earth. She felt dizzy with pleasure from his demanding kiss, from longings he had stirred that made her ache all over.

For an instant the thought flashed in her mind that it wasn't fair. Fate had dealt her a wicked hand. Why did it have to be a man like Cole Chandler, someone she didn't know, an aggravating, arrogant male who laughed at her predicament, charmed and worried her, who could kiss her and drive all reason right out of mind? Worry receded as his hold on her tightened. "You're a green-eyed witch."

"Oh, thanks," she whispered, struggling to regain her control. "What did you say your name is?"

He chuckled, his warm breath brushing her ear. "You know what it is. I think fate brought you to me." His tongue's hot moistness flicked her ear, heightening the scorching giddiness she was already feeling.

"Not fate. A damned, faulty hot-air baloon." *If*

she had consumed a gallon of heady wine, she didn't think it would be any more difficult to concentrate.

She ignored his laugh as his tongue traced across the nape of her neck, then teased her ear. "I'll always have a soft spot in my heart for balloons," he murmured.

She wasn't sure what he had said or how she had answered. All she knew was that his lips were coming closer again, deliciously closer . . . too close.

"Mr. Chandler!"

"Cole." He kissed her throat.

Summoning her wits, her determination, she stepped back out of his arms. The fiery hunger in his blue eyes made her resolve waver, but she knotted her fists, standing firm.

"That's enough!"

His voice was a silky drawl that disturbed her as much as his touch. "No, you know it's not enough." The corners of his mouth raised slowly. "But I'll wait."

"You can't imagine how nervous you're making me. I promised dinner, but . . ."

He held up his hand. "That's right—you promised. I'm not taking you home now."

His hooded eyes were sending a smoldering message that kept her pulse racing like an idling engine. While part of her conversed with him, another level of thought was conscious of his devastating effect and was urging her to yield, to reach out for his strong, tanned arms.

Jolting her even more, he said, "You look torn with indecision. Honey, why don't you make life easy on yourself? Come here . . ." A long arm reached out for her.

His action alarmed her. Too well she pictured his body, remembered its hardness, its warmth. "No! I promised dinner, that's all!"

His voice became soft, so low she could barely hear. "Your kisses are spectacular . . ."

"Thanks, so are yours. Now, we've covered the subject, let's drop it."

"There's nothing to be scared of," he said gently. Sunlight gave a sheen to the smooth oiled muscles of his shoulders and arms. It was an effort to keep her gaze fixed on his face, not to look again at his magnificent body.

"I'm not scared of you."

"I think you're scared of yourself. Have you ever been in love?"

"Yes, and it didn't have a happy ending." The moment she admitted the truth, she wished she could take it back. Now he'd want all the details.

"I'm sorry." He frowned. "Are you divorced?"

"No. It never got that far along. The man I was engaged to after college died before we married."

"I'm sorry," he said again.

Marilee shrugged. "It was a long time ago. He was in Saigon in the diplomatic service. Are you going to take me home now?"

Cole folded his arms across his broad chest and grinned. "You're staying for dinner, remember?"

"You won't change your mind about it?"

"Not a chance. A promise is a promise."

Suddenly, he frowned and looked up. For an instant she wondered what he was doing, then she heard the motor of a light plane.

It was dark blue, flying low, and coming fast. As it swept over the house Cole burst into action, startling Marilee. He lithely jumped over the chaise and snatched something up.

Amazed, she watched as he raised a two-way radio to his mouth. Static sounded, then Cole spoke.

"Bill, can you spot the plane?"

He flipped the switch and a voice came above

the static. "Nope. It's just a dot through binoculars. Pete's calling in now."

Cole switched back. "It's a Cessna, all blue, no markings, headed northeast. Hurry."

A chill shook her as she listened to the conversation. He *was* a gangster. She'd promised to have dinner with a gangster!

He stood with his back to her, one hand on his narrow hips, the black radio clutched in the other while he watched the plane buzz out of sight. She could imagine him dressed all in black with guns slung on both hips. He probably developed muscles to beat up people. She wanted away from him.

Swearing softly, he shook his head as he turned around to look at her.

"Will you take me home, please?" she said, struggling to make her voice sound normal. "I don't want to stay for dinner."

"What's the matter? You're pale as snow. Honey, don't you feel well?"

"Stay away from me." She backed up quickly. "Mr. Chandler . . ."

"Don't you think it's a little late to call me 'Mr'?" he asked dryly, moving silently closer on bare feet. She was grateful that the towel at least was still securely knotted, in spite of his leap over the chaise.

"I don't want to stay for dinner. There's just no future in any further contact between us. Please take me home."

"What brought on this sudden need to go home?"

"It's not sudden. I've felt it ever since I dropped into your pool."

"No, something just changed you." His blue eyes were ice and his voice hardened. "You don't know who was in the plane, do you?"

"In the plane? No, of course, I don't." She sounded as guilty as a thief. His stern features and chilling blue eyes were turning the day into winter. She even felt cold. It must be ninety-five degrees and she was practically shivering.

She decided to humor him. "It's all right. I'll stay for dinner." She tried to make her voice sound light.

He was studying her as if he were trying to come to some conclusion. "You have a lovely home," she added and wished he would quit boring into her with his direct gaze.

"What the hell is going on in your head now?" he said abruptly.

"Oh, nothing. Nothing at all."

He started toward her and she felt like running madly. "Don't come near me."

"Something's bothering you and I'm going to find out what." He strolled up to her to put his strong arms around her.

"I really don't want to pursue this, this friendship."

Ignoring her, he leaned down to kiss her.

It was as devastating as before. Wild tingles sizzled through her. His warm mouth possessed hers relentlessly and he pulled her closer, his bare flesh burning her skin. Suddenly, she was more fearful of a seduction scene than anything else he might do. She had better get herself under control. He was dangerous beyond all belief.

She pushed away and snapped, "I meant that, Cole! You're not going to kiss me again."

His irresistible smile spread as his white teeth flashed. "Now you sound more like yourself. What got into you?"

"I don't like you."

He laughed. "Thanks, honey. Why don't you like me?"

His smile goaded her beyond caution. "I don't associate with men like you."

Grinning, he persisted. "That's an obtuse state-ment. Explain what you mean by that crack, 'men like me.' "

"You know very well what I mean."

"If I'd known, I wouldn't have asked. Come on, out with it."

"I don't care to associate with . . . with unlaw-abiding citizens, namely you."

His eyes widened a moment in surprise, then he threw back his head, laughing heartily.

"Unlaw-abiding citizens! What a statement. That highfalutin description is just what I'd expect from a schoolteacher."

"You have a few other undesirable traits as well. Lump them all together and you're not my brand of candy!"

"Let's get back to this unlaw-abiding citizen business." His expression became serious. "The plane brought this on. Why on earth? I told you I'm a farmer."

"You look as farmerish as I look Eskimoish."

His blue eyes twinkled and she knew he was having fun at her expense again, making another wave of anger erupt inside her.

"Marilee, I *am* a farmer."

"Oh, yes! You keep a two-way radio within reach. You said you have armed guards, a ten-foot fence! You didn't want that plane over your property."

"I think I could enjoy myself for the next hour, but in the interests of promoting our friendship, I'll explain. I have other concerns besides farming. They're as legitimate as your teaching. I have oil wells, a drilling company, and wheat farms."

"Why were you rushing around when the plane flew over?"

His smile faded while a touch of coldness came back to his eyes. "I'm here because of trouble I've been having. My men haven't been able to stop it, so I came to stay awhile. I'm plagued by cattle rustlers."

"Rustlers! This is a wheat farm."

"That's correct, but there's a cattle show coming up in Kansas City over the Fourth of July weekend. I have some prize cattle here, including a very valuable Aberdeen Angus bull I don't want stolen."

She kept her expression bland, even though she doubted every word he'd said. So he startled her by saying, "You don't believe me, do you?" He took her hand, his strong fingers closing over hers. "Come on. I'll show you. Let's go in the house first."

"Who was in the airplane?" she asked, still dubious.

"I don't know. It didn't have any markings to identify it, so I suspect it belonged to rustlers."

"How can they fly without the authorities catching them?"

"They probably own a strip of land somewhere in easy access. They keep the plane out of sight. They can get a quick view of my territory and where everything is, then some night they'll come in a truck and load up any cattle they can catch." He pulled her along in the direction of the house.

"That's awful!"

"So far they've eluded the officers in this area. I've lost some prize cattle, so I decided to spend a few weeks here and see if I can do anything to help. I alerted my men to watch for trouble. Didn't you hear Bill say Pete was calling the sheriff?"

"I heard something about a call, but not who it was to."

He chuckled, probably remembering her assumption that he was a gangster, and she felt uncomfortable. She was acutely aware of his long legs moving beside her, the bare expanses of tanned flesh. As he opened the gate to the fence around the pool, she asked, "Do you ever wear clothes?"

Grinning, he dropped his arms lightly around her shoulders. "It's too hot today."

His answer wasn't reassuring. He held the back screen door open and she entered a high-ceilinged, cool kitchen. She was surprised when a tall, white-haired woman turned and greeted her, and Cole introduced the woman as Jada Whitehurst, his cook. Jada was the first indication that this might be a normal household.

The older woman smiled warmly as Cole introduced Marilee, her eyes growing round when she learned Marilee had arrived in a balloon.

"Miss O'Neil will stay for dinner with us, Jada."

"Fine. We're happy to have you, Marilee."

"Thank you," Marilee said politely.

"I'm going to find her some dry clothes, then show her around." Cole took Marilee's arm and led her through a long hall.

"What does she think of your nudity?" Marilee whispered.

He laughed. "Who, Jada? I'm not nude. I have a towel securely around my middle. Besides, she put diapers on me. I'm Jada's baby."

There was something defensive in his tone. She didn't want to probe further so she walked quietly beside him. The bare wooden floors gleamed with polish and were delightfully cool under her bare feet. Glancing at the living room and dining room, she saw both had immense fireplaces, heavy dark masculine-style furniture. They climbed a flight of stairs and turned down the hall to enter a bedroom.

"There's a clothes dryer in the utility room down-stairs if you want to use it," Cole said. "Maybe you can wear my sister's clothes. She keeps some things here." He opened a closet door, then glanced back at Marilee whose expression was clearly skeptical. "Hey! She is my sister."

"I didn't say a word nor do I care what female clothing is in your bedroom."

She saw the wicked gleam in his blue eyes and braced herself for some of his devilment. He held up his hand. "I swear, they're my sister's clothes. She spends some weekends here. And you don't have to say anything. Disapproval is flashing in your green eyes."

"That's not so! We have no attachment to each other. We're strangers . . ."

"Ahhh, strangers? After the kisses we shared?"

She blushed and hated it. "I'll find something to wear."

"There's a connecting bath. My room is across the hall. Want to see it?"

"Not really."

He chuckled. "Take your time. When you get changed, come downstairs. I'll be waiting. After we eat I'll show you Bonny Charles."

"Who's Bonny Charles?"

"Bonny Charles of Argyle. He's my prize Angus." He started out of the room. "If you need help with a zipper or anything . . ."

"I won't need your help!"

He laughed again as he crossed the room to the door. Unbidden, as she watched muscles ripple in his tanned back, she recalled her first glimpse of him, of his fit, male body. Instead of leaving the room, he suddenly glanced over his shoulder, catching her studying him.

There was no way to stop the warmth flooding her cheeks again. He tilted his head, his expression altering slightly. He turned around to face her, his brown fingers resting on the white towel over his hips.

"Sure you don't want my help?" he said, his voice low.

"Thank you, no. Definitely not."

When his gaze went over her once again in a thorough, lingering appraisal that made her cheeks continue to burn, she said, "I hope there's a dress with a high neck and long sleeves in the closet."

He smiled. "In this Kansas heat, I doubt if my sister brought any such dress here. But, if she did—my memory's good."

The twinkle in his blue eyes was impossible to resist and she laughed. "Do you ever let up?"

"I can't. I'm overcome. I've never met anyone like you."

"Oh, no, I'm sure you haven't!"

"I haven't. It's the first time someone has come down into my pool in a hot-air balloon. You've amused me, you're luscious, delightful to kiss—"

"Thank you," she said quickly.

"And you need help. . . ."

"With what?"

"Your dreadful hang-ups."

"No, thanks a million anyway. I can imagine your methods of help. I don't have a bunch of hang-ups. I'm the normal one."

He chuckled, turning to go. "See you downstairs."

As soon as he was gone, she crossed the room to close the door. Sighing with relief, she gazed around the spacious room. A high ceiling and wide windows proclaimed the house's age. The room was furnished in white, and even the four-poster bed had a white organdy canopy above a frilly white spread. Pink carpet covered the floor. It was obviously a woman's room. She wondered if his sister really did stay here.

She pulled the long cord to turn on a ceiling fan, watching the blades slowly rotate, stirring a breeze. Both windows were open and she strolled over to one to look out. She was facing north, away from the pool. There was a wide fenced yard, a road running in front of it, then golden wheat spreading away to the flat, distant horizon. To her right she saw some of the outbuildings, a shed and the red roof of the barn.

She moved to the closet and studied the half-dozen dresses hanging there, trying first one, then another until she selected a sundress.

An hour later she was bathed. Her hair had been washed and dried and was shining with glistening highlights. It fell loosely over her shoulders, swinging slightly with each step. Tied over each shoulder with spaghetti straps, the green cotton sundress had a full skirt that swirled against her bare, tanned legs. It was slightly long, but it fit otherwise and was cool enough for the hot Kansas summer. The sandals she had found were a size too large, but adequate, and Marilee walked carefully down the stairs. She was almost at the bottom when Cole appeared, standing with his arms akimbo, watching her descent.

He looked so handsome! The magnetism that hovered between them struck her with a tingling awareness, making her pulse gallop. Her gaze ran over him and she was surprised to see a white apron partially covering his pale blue knit shirt and dark slacks.

Appraising her in return, he whistled appreciatively.

She missed her step. As she started to tumble down the stairs, she grabbed at the banister. Cole's strong arms caught her and she blushed furiously as she looked up at him, silently cursing the awkward, too-large sandals.

"Thank you."

He continued to hold her against his chest. "I should've whistled sooner."

She wriggled free, keeping her voice calm. "It's the shoes. Are you helping Jada cook dinner?"

"Nope, I gave Jada the evening off. Come on. I'll fix you a drink and you can watch me cook."

Walking cautiously to keep the sandals on her feet, she followed him to the kitchen. It was old-fashioned but equipped with modern appliances. The cabinets had glass fronts, but the countertop was white Formica. The woodwork was also white and pots of flowers hung in the south and east windows.

Cole looked in the oven. "Potatoes are baking but it'll be awhile before they're ready. We'll eat on the patio because it's cooler and I can grill steaks outside."

While he knelt down to pull a pan out of a drawer, she noted how his slacks molded his strong legs. He straightened and caught her watching him, and she turned away to hide what she suspected might be revealed in her face.

"Marilee."

His voice was low, seductive, sending an insidious shiver from head to toe. She heard his boots strike the floor, then his hands were on her shoulders and he turned her to face him. A thick lock of brown hair curled over his forehead and she fought the urge to smooth it back. "There is something special between us," he said in a husky voice.

Exhaling slowly, she gazed up at him. "Cole, don't rush me."

"I'm not."

"Keep your mind on cooking."

"How can I?" He smiled. "The best dish in the house has red hair." He kissed the tip of her nose and his voice returned to normal. "What would you like to drink? A glass of red wine?"

"Yes, please. Can I help?"

"Come here." He took her arm and led her outside to the patio. It was shaded by sycamores and had rough oak chairs and a table, and a chaise with bright orange cushions. Another high stake fence gave them complete privacy.

"You have a thing about fences, don't you?"

He shrugged. "I value my privacy." He stopped by one of the chairs. "You sit down here. I'll bring your wine and join you in a second."

After he went inside, she looked around. A trail of tempting hickory smoke rose from a black grill. The table was set for two with lovely crystal and china that looked slightly incongruous on the patio.

Other than the song of a bird, it was still, so peaceful. She sat quietly relaxed while a slight breeze cooled her. It had been a strange day and she still felt dazed, as if in shock. This morning seemed years away.

Cole pushed open the door, interrupting her reverie. Carrying a basket of bread, he stepped outside, his gaze lowered as he crossed the patio. The apron was gone. He walked with an easy grace, his broad shoulders swinging slightly. The vivid image sprang to mind of his muscular, nude body, the mat of dark hair covering his chest. When he sat down facing her, knees almost touching, his blue eyes levelled on her, she felt a tightening in her midriff.

"What're you thinking?" Cole murmured.

She feigned casualness. "Not much."

In a mocking drawl, he said, "I haven't known you twenty-four hours, but I know that answer is pure bull."

"I'm not about to tell you what's on my mind."

"Let me guess . . ."

"No!"

He laughed. "That bad, eh?"

"Not at all. I can just imagine your suggestive guesses."

"Do you know how pink your cheeks are?"

"That's a redhead's curse."

"I think it's delightful. It goes with your green eyes." He smiled and handed her a glass of wine before holding his out in a toast. "Here's to our future."

"How can I drink to that?"

"It's easy. Raise your glass."

Relenting, she smiled also and touched his glass lightly with hers.

"I want to get to know you," he said after he sipped the wine. "You said you teach. What age children?"

"All ages. I've taught remedial reading in grades two through twelve. This year I'm teaching high school."

"Do you often see quick results or are the results long-range?"

"That's the thrill of my work. It's the most marvelous feeling in the world to see children change, to see them grasp the printed word, master a skill most of them thought impossible."

He rested his chin on his hand, leaning close to her while he listened to the enthusiasm in her voice. After sipping her wine, she continued. "I've worked out methods of my own and I've written a textbook."

"Hey, that's pretty good!"

"I'm pleased. It's been adopted in some Wichita high schools this year and—"

"Your eyes seem a deeper green than this afternoon," he interrupted in a soft voice.

A warmth slithered down her spine. "It's this green dress that does it."

"I interrupted you. Go ahead. And . . . ?"

For an instant she stared at him blankly, trying to remember what she had been telling him. "Oh. Next year more schools will use my text. A high school in Arkansas City will have it and two in Topeka." While she talked he scooted closer and reached out to brush a tendril of hair from her shoulder. Suddenly she had difficulty concentrating on her conversation. She'd had three sips of wine, yet she had a giddy feeling that was short-circuiting her thought processes. "I'm writing a second text now."

"I think that's great! You must be good at teaching reading." His eyes narrowed thoughtfully. "My nephew has difficulty reading." His hand rested on her shoulder, his flesh warm against her own, and he toyed with the ends of her hair.

"Has he been tested for dyslexia, problems of that sort?" She tried to control a shiver as his fingers brushed the sensitive skin behind her ear.

"Yep. He just doesn't want to read, he doesn't like it."

She studied his amazingly thick, curly eyelashes, his strong jaw and prominent cheekbones. "He probably doesn't like reading because he can't do it. How old is he?"

"Eight." He swished strands of her hair over her shoulder, tickling her skin, making it increasingly difficult to breathe.

"He's young. Usually the younger the student, the easier he is to help."

"Oh, you slipped there. Aren't there any 'she's'—any girls?"

"Of course not! We're far quicker than the male."

He laughed, making creases deepen around his

mouth and lines fan out from the corners of his eye. "The female—superior of the species."

"Naturally. Little girls come into the world with brains going full steam."

"All set on ensnaring a male."

She laughed. "Now you slipped," she said with a laugh. "You revealed your feelings about women." Sobering, she caught his hand. "This belongs here." She removed it from her shoulder and placed it carefully on the arm of his chair.

He immediately raised it again to trace her jaw. "Why? You don't like my touch?"

"I lose my train of thought."

His gaze moved leisurely over her features, lingering on her lips while his voice became husky. "Isn't that a coincidence? I have the same reaction." With each word he leaned closer and her pulse jumped wildly. His lips met hers, brushing, teasing, then taking hers fully. If anything, his kiss was more dazzling than it had been in the afternoon. The erotic tingles exploding from his demanding mouth set off a roar in her ears.

She dimly felt him remove the glass of wine from her hand. He rose and slipped his arm around her waist. He lifted her easily and sat down with her on his lap. For a brief moment she yielded, running her fingers across the strong column of his throat, winding them in the thick, soft hair that curled at the nape of his neck.

Like snatching at leaves in a high wind, she gathered her wits, pushing away and rising to slip back into her chair. "You don't waste any time, do you?" she asked in a shaky voice.

His expression was solemn, intent. "I can't help what I feel when I touch you."

Her insides would definitely be out of kilter if he didn't stop. "Slow down a little!"

He sipped his wine, still gazing at her with

piercing, stormy blue eyes. His tone was another caress. "You drop out of the blue into my life, working a magic spell over me, witch."

"I'm not doing anything to you," she answered, wishing she didn't sound so breathless. When his slow smile refuted her words thoroughly, she added, "Maybe you've been isolated here too long."

He studied her thoughtfully. "It's summertime, you'll be here to paint my house—"

"I didn't agree to take the job!" Earlier, she had even thought his offer was a joke.

"I'll make you a deal too good to turn down."

"You might be surprised. Sometimes I do have some resistance." But not to that charming smile, she thought.

"If"—he stressed the word heavily, pausing a moment—"you paint the house, you'll be around all day anyway. Would you consider tutoring my nephew for an hour each afternoon? You'll be paid for that, too." He grinned. "It won't be thrown in with the painting."

"Does he live near you?"

"He's close enough. It'll be convenient."

"Your sister lives on the farm too?"

"We're just plain farm folks."

"I have another week before school is out for the summer."

"I can wait a week."

She didn't want to paint his house. He was too aggressive; she was too vulnerable. There was a current of attraction between them that was startling and compelling.

"What are you thinking?"

"That I should avoid you."

"Oh? Am I threatening?"

"I won't tell you. Your ego is far too large now."

"Aw, shucks. Under this cool, assured exterior might be a timid, shy heart."

"I'll believe it when I see a shred of evidence pointing that way."

She was subjected to his engaging smile again. "If I were certain of myself, I'd take you into my arms again." His voice was husky, teasing with a hint of laughter. "The only thing that stops me is the fear of rejection. Otherwise, I'd put my fingers on your soft throat, touch your gorgeous red hair, taste your lips . . ."

She wriggled in an unconscious movement that wasn't lost on him. "Stop right now! I'm rejecting you," she teased.

He threw up his hands while he settled back in the chair. "See, I told you. I'm very timid."

She laughed and they were silent a moment before he returned to the earlier topic. "What about helping Henry an hour each day? Will you do it?"

She was back to the same decision. She could far more easily reject the offer to paint his house than she could reject trying to help his nephew. Every child was different, each a unique challenge.

"First, don't you think you should confer with his mother?"

"She'd be delighted if she thought you would help. Henry was off to a bad start his first year in school. They moved constantly and he was shuffled from one school to another. What's the going rate for tutoring?"

When she told him, he offered to double it. "Why the enormous fee?" she asked, surprised. "Your offer has overtones of calculated persuasion."

"Might be." His blue eyes seemed to be daring her. "You don't paint alone, do you?"

"No, two teachers help me. We're unemployed in the summer, you know."

"You don't get a salary?"

"Not all summer."

"This should be a good job. Will you take it?"

"Don't you want an estimate first?" She was stalling, snatching at straws, prolonging what she knew was coming, what she couldn't resist doing. She felt as if she had tumbled into a vat of blue, deep cerulean blue as she gazed into eyes that wouldn't release her.

"You can give me an estimate tomorrow."

"On Sunday?"

"I'm sure we can work out the details. Will you do it?"

She thought of her two helpers who were in need of funds. It would be absurd not to accept the job, especially if she were here anyway to tutor his nephew. But to be constantly around Cole . . . Her pulse started climbing while little red flags of warning popped into her mind. Another heartbreak, and one had been enough. Could she avoid hurt if she stayed in daily contact with a man whose mere look set her pulses racing? While he quietly waited for her answer, she felt as if she were drowning in blue eyes and all she could think was danger, danger. "All right, I will."

"Good. That's settled."

"To your satisfaction."

He leaned forward swiftly, slipping his hand across the back of her neck to pull her closer to him. Her heart was pounding in her ears.

"You're a delight to look at, to hold, to touch."

She tried to keep control. "Cole, please don't complicate my life. It's very orderly and peaceful."

"I won't cause trouble. That isn't my intention at all." A lopsided grin tugged at the corner of his mouth. "I saw an example today of how orderly and peaceful your life is."

"That was the fault of the balloon. Very exceptional. You can't imagine how quiet and ordinary my life is."

"You betcha, hon. Want to walk down to the corral and see Bonny Charles?"

"Sure." Anything to get away before he discovered how fast her heart was racing. She promised herself firmly that she would resist his charms. He rose and reached down to pull her to her feet.

Three

She came up into his arms. Without warning, he kissed her. Her promise to resist Cole vanished. She knew her quiet life was threatened by a hurricane of passion unless she was careful, but she couldn't worry about it anymore. He destroyed every thought but that she wanted him.

Slowly, he released her and they stood immobile, looking at each other. Cole's arm tightened around her waist and he lowered his head to repeat the kiss.

In desperation she asked, "What about Bonny Charles or whatever his name is?"

There was only a moment's hesitation before he smiled and stepped away. "Come along. It'll be time to put the steaks on when we get back."

While her pulse rate simmered, they strolled along a gravel drive past a fenced, neatly trimmed green yard, a startling contrast to the desert of wheat. Between open, weed-filled stretches of land, the drive curved away from the house to the fenced areas around the barn and sheds. As they circled the barn to a pen behind it, Marilee was totally conscious of Cole's nearness, his long legs moving beside her, his shoulder occasionally brushing hers. She was relieved when they reached the pen and she could concentrate on the majestic black bull standing by the fence. As they approached, he blew air in a low snort.

"Bonny Charles, this is Miss Marilee O'Neil. Marilee, meet Bonny Charles of Argyle."

She stared into the bull's soft brown eyes. He flicked a black ear and switched his tail while she climbed up on the fence and leaned over to rub her hand down his sleek nose.

"He's beautiful," she said, a little awed. "Look at his brown eyes. You're not going to eat him, are you?"

Cole laughed. "No, ma'am, I'm sure not going to eat Bonny Charles. He's going to earn me a nice sum of money."

She studied the ring through his nose. "Doesn't that ring hurt him?"

"No. It keeps him docile when he's led around."

Slipping his arm around her waist, Cole swung her off the fence. He held her tightly against him, her toes just above the ground, her hands resting on his shoulders, and she thought again of how his hard, lean body had looked by the pool. "You're blushing again," he said in a low voice. "Remembering this afternoon? Our kiss by the pool?"

"I can't forget," she answered simply.

He groaned and started to lower his head, but she turned slightly. "Cole, alarms are going off inside my mind like firecrackers on the Fourth of July. You're 'danger' in mile-high letters."

"Why?"

She focused on the locks of brown hair that the

wind was tugging off his forehead. "I told you, I have a neatly planned, orderly life. And I seem to have very bad luck when it comes to men."

"A kiss is so dangerous?"

He asked the question lightly, but his words hung in the air, pulling tautly at her. Her soft breasts were pressed into his chest, her fingers rested at the base of his throat. Easily, she detected a pulse racing as fast as her own.

"Incredibly dangerous!" she whispered.

"When you give me an answer like that, little witch, what do you think I have to do?" he replied just before his mouth possessed hers.

The firecrackers changed to rockets. Red, blue, green, fabulous blinding colors, spinning, sizzling, exploding inside her, setting her ablaze. She longed to slide her arms across his broad shoulders, to wrap them around him and cling to him. His kiss burned through her. When she finally managed to wriggle free, she realized this kiss was far more difficult to stop than the one before, and the one before that. She stepped back with a shaky laugh. "A ring in the nose for Bonny Charles, a kiss for me—that's all it takes to make us docile."

"Docile?" he drawled as his gaze lowered to her breasts, which were thrusting against the green cotton, her taut peaks outlined.

"You promised dinner." She tried to sound forceful.

"I'm hungry too, but not for steak."

Trying to change the subject, to bank the smoldering flames in his blue eyes, she asked, "Don't you feel a little guilty talking about steaks in front of him?"

For a moment his gaze continued to hold hers, then he smiled. "No, he didn't bat an eye." He took her hand and they turned back to the house.

Her nerves felt raw and she was too conscious

of his nearness. In an attempt to give herself a chance to recover, she asked, "Where do you stay when you're not here?"

"I have a home and an office in Tulsa, Oklahoma. Later, around the end of July, I'm going to Alaska. We're drilling for oil. I'll spend at least six weeks up there."

Was there a woman waiting for him in Tulsa, in Alaska? That line of thought was too unsettling and she concentrated on his warm hand, lightly holding hers.

"I haven't shown you the house," he said. "After a while we'll take a tour."

"Is this where you grew up?"

"Part of the time. My parents were divorced. Sandy, my sister, and I were shuffled back and forth between them."

He stated it flatly as if it were of little consequence to him, but she wondered if he really felt that unconcerned. She thought of her own parents who lived in Wichita about a mile away from her. "Your life must've been difficult."

"It was difficult for them. Neither of our parents wanted to take us. They're not alive anymore."

Surprised, she tried to keep her features passive. His answer explained the defensiveness in his voice when he had talked about Jada earlier.

"How old were you when they divorced?"

"Eleven and Sandy was eight."

"That's tough."

"My dad was busy with his job and my mother moved to California for an acting career. She wasn't successful at it, but she didn't want two kids cluttering up her life."

As Marilee listened, she compared his background to hers. Her family enjoyed one another. She couldn't imagine the situation he described. She glanced at his jaw clamped shut though, and knew she shouldn't offer sympathy. Instead, she said, "You and your sister must be close."

"We are. When I was sixteen, Dad died. I came back here to live for four years until Sandy could go to college."

"Did you get to go?"

There was no mistaking the note of steel in his tone as he replied, "I put a mortgage on the farm and went to college at the same time. I majored in geology."

"How did you get into the drilling business?"

"After graduation I started working for an oil company. I found an area where I felt certain we'd hit oil, but no one was interested. I'd already learned how to borrow money when I went to college. I rounded up some investors, borrowed more, drilled, and was lucky."

"Lucky? You mean you were right."

They walked in silence a moment before he said gruffly, "I'm not the marrying kind."

His unexpected statement pierced like a dagger and anger flooded through her. He was the one who had made the passes, not she. She stopped in her tracks to face him. "Why not?"

He was startled and emotions flickered over his features. The shuttered look vanished, dissolving into surprise. His narrowed brows flew upward, his eyes widened, then a twinkle appeared.

He laughed. "That's the first time anyone has asked in quite so direct a manner."

The first time! "I rather resent your announcement! You come on to me with the persistence of a flock of starving vultures and then have the gall to inform me that it won't ever mean anything to you if I succumb!" She tapped his chest with her forefinger, and his eyes danced with glee. "What you're actually saying is you don't want commitment in a relationship! Well, we don't have a relationship and we're not going to have one!"

He chuckled. "Just wanted you to know . . ."

"So I wouldn't get my hopes up! Pzzz! What an ego!" She poked his chest again, ignoring his grin. "Let me tell you, Cole Chandler, I don't take relationships lightly! Be ye warned, too, my friend!"

His hearty laughter floated over the field. He reached out, wrapping her in his embrace, pulling her to him for a hug. When he released her, he looked down at her. The impact of those blue eyes jarred her more than she cared to admit. One corner of his mouth tugged upward in another lopsided grin. "Also, that's the first time my technique has been likened to starving vultures! I may be losing my touch."

She pushed away, but he caught her around the waist. "Come on, witch. I'll feed you and see if I can't soften you up." His fingers trailed over the curve of her derrière. "But then, you're pretty soft as it is . . ."

"Cole!" She wiggled impatiently, shaking off his hand. "See what I mean about starving vultures?"

He laughed, then his amusement vanished. "I can't resist. There's an attraction that makes me want to grab you and hold you . . ." He sounded puzzled.

Everything—heart, brain, breath—seemed to stop. With enormous effort, she turned away. "We better find something safer to do. How about dinner?"

"If you say so." He replaced his arm around her waist until they entered the enclosed patio and she sat down to watch while he put thick, red steaks on the smoking grill. As he stood over the cooker, she gazed at his tanned arms with their sprinkling of short dark hair and thought about the past few minutes. Why the curt announcement? She hadn't made a claim on him; she barely knew him. With a shock she realized it felt as if she had known Cole forever. The attraction between them was so right, so compelling, it seemed more than momentary. It was monumental.

Whatever his reason, the statement was a clear warning. And not just about marriage. It included commitment, any lasting hold. It was an announcement that part of him was private and wouldn't be shared. She crossed her slender legs, watching him move, his long frame so masculine, so appealing, so capable of wounding her if she let him. He looked up and his blue eyes met hers with the impact of gale winds. She felt buffeted, absorbed by a bit of blue. He winked and she smiled, forgetting her warning to herself.

They ate companionably, relishing the juicy steaks. Afterward they carried the dishes to the kitchen, then Cole took her on a tour of the house.

Down the long hall they entered the dining room with a massive mahogany table and carved chairs. Masculine, elegant, the furnishings suited his personality. Next they went into the living room, filled with more dark furniture. One entire wall was covered with weapons.

Marilee halted and gazed at the guns, knives, and miscellaneous objects of mayhem. "You must like violence."

"No, I find weapons interesting, so I collect them. I don't use them," he added dryly.

She moved closer. "I don't like guns. If they'd never been invented, think what the world might've been."

He chuckled. "Probably uninhabited. undefended, men would've killed each other off with stones and rocks."

"You have a bec de corbin, and a jousting helmet . . . I can't imagine people actually using such things." She glanced at him to find him staring at her intently.

"How do you know a bec de corbin?"

"My father's a gun collector. I've read about these in his books."

"And he's a violent man?"

"I deserved that one." She laughed. "Somehow it seems different with you. He doesn't have all the other weapons."

Cole reached out to tuck her hair behind her ear, letting his finger trail down her cheek. His touch was lighter than a summer breeze, yet it made her tingle. His fingertips made her aware of the silence around them, the intimacy of their closeness in the empty house. She sidled a few feet away to view more of the collection. "You have two powder horns decorated with maps! My dad has tried to find one. He has two Kentucky rifles he values. One's a Jacob Dickert."

"I'd like to see your father's collection."

"He'd love to show it to you. He spends hours over it." She shivered. "I don't like guns."

He stood on his toes and removed a large pistol from a high shelf. "This one's loaded."

Horror-struck, she gazed at the weapon in his hand. "You keep a loaded gun here?"

"This is for emergencies. It's too high for kids to reach. It's no use to have one that isn't loaded. Look here." He broke it open, removing the cartridges. Snapping it closed, he released the safety. "All you do is pull the hammer to cock it and squeeze the trigger."

His blunt, tanned finger squeezed the trigger. The gun clicked and he held it out to her. "Try it."

Chilled, she rubbed her arms. Cole looked perfectly natural handling the gun, but she didn't want any part of it. "No, thanks. I don't need a gun in my line of work."

He reloaded and replaced the weapon, his shirt stretching tautly over his arm and back while he reached upward. Turning back to her with a smile, he said, "Let's go sit on the patio."

She chose the chair she'd sat in earlier. He pulled his beside hers and propped his booted feet up on the edge of another chair.

Night had come with a full moon. It was a cool summer evening filled with the lingering smell of woodsmoke from the smoldering grill. Overhead stars twinkled brilliantly, hundreds more visible in the clear country air than in town. It was beautiful, but filled with danger. Marilee knew now was the time to ask Cole to take her home, to walk out of his life and see him only for professional reasons when she came to paint and tutor. Instead she sat in silence, every nerve alive to the slightest movement, the simplest touch of the man beside her. Only several kisses had passed between them, nothing more. She could easily forget them she told herself, ignoring a jeering little voice in her mind that laughed contemptuously.

"What are you thinking about?" he asked.

If he only knew! "It's nice here."

"I know." His voice was a deep rumble in the dark. He reached over to take her hand, his warm fingers closing around hers. "I like it here. This is the only place that's really home to me."

"When you were growing up, did you spend much time here?"

"About half my life. Especially the early years. When my parents fought, I could get away from them and not hear the angry words."

"I'm sorry."

"That was long ago. I seldom even give it thought anymore. It doesn't seem very real to me now. I used to sleep outside when I was a kid. The patio wasn't fenced and you could watch the sun come up. Dawn is beautiful in summertime."

She settled back in her chair, gazing at the stars, surprised that Cole would enjoy just sitting quietly.

After a time he asked her, "What's your father do?"

"He retired last year from his job as a pharmaceutical salesman."

"Do you have any brothers or sisters?"

"Yes, five sisters."

"I'll bet your father's spoiled rotten."

She laughed. "He might be at that. I've never seen him cook anything."

"I can't remember learning," Cole remarked. His thumb moved back and forth over the back of her hand, tickling lightly, making her acutely aware of his proximity, his touch.

"Want something to drink?"

"No, thanks."

He scooted closer, dropping his right arm around her shoulder, taking her fingers in his left hand.

She was ready to protest if he turned to kiss her, but he settled back to gaze at the sky. Somewhere in the distance a forlorn howl drifted through the night. Close at hand, dogs barked an answer.

Marilee listened, wondering what it would be like to grow up in the country, to live in a big house as Cole had. She tried to visualize what he would have looked like as a small boy. Instead, into her mind flashed the enticing image of his lean tanned body at poolside, his blue eyes dancing.

With the lightness of a breeze, his fingers grazed the back of her neck, then drifted across her shoulder and along her upper arm. The swift singing current that raced in her veins was enough to bring her to her feet.

"Cole, I need to get home," she announced firmly. He stood beside her and placed his palms on her shoulders, the knit sleeves of his blue shirt tightening around his biceps.

Ignoring the heated touch of his hands, she brought up the subject she had managed to avoid all evening. "I want to take Jack's balloon home. I don't want you to buy a new one."

"I've already told him to buy one and that I'd pay for it. I don't go back on my word."

"You're making the inevitable more difficult."

In a soft voice, he drawled, "Here's the inevitable—and I've waited much too long."

Her mouth felt dry while the hammering in her ears almost drowned out the sound of his voice. He reached out, pulling her into his arms. His smile vanished as his voice deepened. "This is as certain as the wheat turning gold beneath the Kansas sun."

When he leaned down to kiss her, taking her mouth and stopping her mild protest, she knew she had made a mistake. She should have asked him to take her home the moment dinner was over. The thought faded into oblivion, driven away by total awareness of Cole, his mouth, his lean frame.

He parted her lips, invading her mouth with an assurance that confirmed his words. Why did his kiss have to feel right? So exciting? Finally, she pushed away slightly to whisper, "We shouldn't. I shouldn't. Not now. Please . . ."

"Shh, witch." His mouth brushed hers lightly. "No negative statements, no rejection. Not between us."

"Cole, I want this to end, finish. Period."

He shook his head. "Impossible. You're an enchantress, an auburn-haired Circe who's bewitched me." Once more his lips feathered over hers, melting her resistance.

The lightest brush of his mouth was electrifying, tripping the hammers, revving the tiny motors to send steamheat boiling in her blood. His lips pressed hers eagerly, parting them to give him access to her mouth. She was held fast in his arms while his tongue demanded her response, the sweet, fiery clash that raised temperatures instantly.

His lips trailed kisses to her throat, overwhelming her. Her bones melted. Her lashes dropped as she sought his lips for another incredible kiss that would sweep her beyond logic.

While one strong arm held her about the waist, the fingertips of his other hand drifted across her neck, over her bare shoulder, down, down across the thin cotton covering her breast.

She gasped and twisted. "Cole, leave me some peace! I don't want this . . ."

"You don't want my mouth here?" His lips brushed the soft curve of her full breast. He held her still while his fingers trailed lower over her hip. Kiss for kiss, input matched output. She couldn't stop. Throbbing sensation was sending the voltage to dangerous levels.

His mouth, his hands, made her tingling body clamor for attention. Steadily, his wandering fingers and fiery kisses were overloading her system, obliterating every thought for survival. She had known from the start, from the first tempestuous kiss, that she was lost to him.

It had been so long since she had been passionately loved. She was achingly vulnerable and she knew it, but the knowledge was useless. She felt ambushed, unable or unwilling to protest.

He held her close, leaning over, bending her body under his. His long legs pressed against hers and she felt his maleness. One hand roamed up the curve of her spine, caressing, sliding down to the small of her back. His fingers moved slowly to the nape of her neck, massaging her lightly, starting a shower of fire.

"Cole, I don't know you. . . ." she agonized.

"Hush, woman. This is magic, it's fire meeting fire. We complete each other. . . ."

Shifting her in his arms, he kissed her again. One of his hands brushed across her breast, caressing a taut peak. She arched her back instinctively at his touch and whimpered, the sound muffled by his mouth on hers.

Cole, almost a stranger, became something else, someone needed, another part of herself. The breathtaking hunger he had awakened escalated to an urgency that made her writhe. His rough fingertips slipped beneath a thin strap, sliding it over her shoulder, pushing the green cotton down carefully, his gaze following the material.

Closing her eyes, she tilted her head, her hair swinging lightly over her bare shoulders as his fingers slipped the other strap down with slow deliberation. The faintest rustle of material drifted over her trembling body as he pushed the sundress to her waist, baring her breasts to his appreciative gaze. His forefinger and thumb teased her hardened nipple, then his mouth sought her breast. His dark brown hair brushed against her, its softness tormenting while his tongue abolished her reluctance.

The chemistry of attraction between them was volatile. Overpowered with desire, she felt weak in the knees. Never in her life had a man been able to arouse her so swiftly, so completely. He rained kisses over her tender, pale breasts, across her throat while his hands continued stroking her, caressing her back, the nape of her neck.

All rational thought was gone. She was swept into a vortex of passion. Urgency racked her, intensifying to desperate longing. Her hips arched against him.

"That's it, Marilee," Cole murmured. "Touch me, love me."

Sliding her hands over his strong back and powerful muscles, she traced his sharp shoulder blades, roving down to his narrow waist. "Cole . . ." she began.

"Shh, honey. You're a golden girl. You have a warm, golden body. With your beautiful red hair you're like a goddess, a sorceress. So lovely, so desirable."

Each word was a stroke, smoothing away loneliness, erasing disappointment and fear, heightening an emotional need that was as strong as the physical. "Pure nonsense," she managed to whisper, even as she clung to him. "You're ridiculous. I'm a plain, ordinary schoolteacher."

He kissed her throat. "Something happens between us when we touch, you know that." In the silvery moonlight his blue eyes held her spellbound while he whispered, "This is destiny. I'm never here at this time of year. How often have you crashed a balloon?"

He didn't wait for her to answer. His mouth conquered her protests his plundering tongue making her senses clamor for more. Ablaze, she returned his kisses with unbridled eagerness, her tongue meeting his. Hot, intimate, each clash set wild tingles racing.

Her response was primordial, timeless. Craving exploded, spreading its fury, compelling her to yield. He moved away briefly to pull his shirt over his head and drop it on the ground. Moonlight splashed across his dark chest, highlighting his muscled shoulders, the powerful biceps. He bent his head to kiss her breast, cupping it gently in his large hand.

She groaned in anguish. "We mustn't do this!"

"Of course not," he breathed over her bare midriff. Singeing forays of his tongue built a conflagration that burned insistently.

Like candlelight in a blizzard, her protests were suddenly extinguished. His fingers pushed down the sundress. He knelt, slacks pulling tautly over his knees and thighs while his hands rested on her hips, holding her.

She swayed as his intense gaze took in all of her golden body, especially the blurred triangle of red-gold curls, half-hidden by her flimsy white lace panties. The sight of his dark hands on her pale skin enflamed her beyond reason. It didn't matter that she scarcely knew Cole Chandler, that he was in her life only temporarily, that he could hurt her. She wanted him . . . now.

"You know this is special," he said as if in answer to her thoughts. He spoke with a breathlessness that made her feel as if she were the only woman in the world for him.

Rising, he wrapped his arms around her to kiss her again, his mouth reaffirming his words, heightening her desire.

His furred chest met her sensitive breasts, making her draw a deep breath. He swept her into his arms then laid her down on the chaise. In a lithe movement he stretched out beside her and pulled her against his hard length. She was drowning in sensation and mindlessly wrapped her arms around him.

In the moonlight his blue eyes devoured her. His lower lip was full and sensuous, red from her kisses. "Have you ever, with any other man, felt what you feel with me?" he demanded huskily.

She didn't want to admit the truth. Her reaction to him wasn't logical . . . but it was real. She felt the magnetism between them in every pore. While she mulled it over, the burning desire in his eyes made her ache. He didn't have to touch her to get a response, to have a devastating effect on her.

Persisting, he said, "Answer me, Marilee. I want to hear you say it. I already see the answer in your eyes. When I look at your mouth, your lips part. You respond to me just as I do to you."

"I shouldn't," she whispered, even as her skin tingled whenever it was pressed against his own naked flesh.

"Ah, yes. And I respond to you. You look at my mouth like you just did and I feel as though I'm going to burst with my need for you. I can't stop now. Together, we're extraordinary. The passion that explodes between us when we touch is fabulous. It is to me."

"You're not fair," she said breathlessly. "You've cheated me, blackmailed me into dinner. . . ."

He brushed her lips with his.

Ignoring the scalding sensation of his mouth, she turned her head to continue the charges. "You're seducing me. . . ."

"You like this."

"You won't listen. . . ."

She gasped, her fingers biting into his shoulder as he kissed her throat.

"I'm listening to every word. Tell me you don't want this, honey." His head drooped forward to kiss the valley between her breasts.

"Cole, oh please!"

His gaze locked with hers. He sat up and tugged off his boots, his socks. He rose, unfastening his heavy silver belt buckle. She felt unable to move as she watched each unhurried movement of his hands. He unfastened the dark slacks, letting them fall, revealing his unforgettable body, bronzed, muscled, so male. A triangle of black underwear was peeled away. Cole was as nude as when she first saw him, only now he was fully aroused, ready for her.

She longed to reach out, to touch his smooth copper flesh. Her fingertips, as if of their own volition, drifted over a solid, hard thigh, through short, curling hairs. She heard him gasp as he sank down, stretching out to pull her against him. One arm pinned her to him as his mouth seized hers.

His hand began stroking her long, silky legs, making her writhe with uncontrollable desire. His fingers traveled over her intimately, exploring her moist warmth. She gasped, crying a muffled protest as his bold fingers moved insidiously to arouse her to a frenzied peak.

And then he brought her over the brink, beyond the point of return. There were no more protests, no denials. She was consumed with a yearning for him, a desperate longing to encompass his hard male body.

Her kisses conveyed her frantic urgency, driving him to the edge of turbulent desire. Before his lovemaking had been devastating; now it was like wildfire. Her restraint burned away like flaming dry leaves. She wanted to wrap her arms around him and hold him forever.

"Ahh, sweet witch, you're magic to me! I can't get enough. I want to make you want me as badly as I do you."

"Cole!" She squirmed with ravenous hunger and he eased her onto her back.

She was aware of the rough canvas of the chaise against her bare skin while she watched wide-eyed as Cole moved over her. Locks of his brown hair hung on his forehead and his temples. A sheen of perspiration made his skin glow. With each movement, the muscles in his back rippled beneath her hands. His knee pushed her legs apart and he came down above her, holding his weight off her.

Her limbs felt heavy. She quivered with undisguised longing, wanting him, needing him beyond anything she imagined possible. Every brush against his strong arms, his flat stomach, made her desire him more. Leaning down, he kissed her hotly while she arched her hips to receive him.

Penetration made her cry out, a muffled sound smothered by his kiss. He continued relentlessly, taking her in strokes that carried them both on a rising current of sensation. The first moment of pain had disappeared and ecstasy burst within her. Pleasure and need were one, generating a hot flood of passion.

"Now, little green-eyed witch . . ." Cole said, his lips on her ear. "Now, I'll make you mine . . ."

She barely heard him. No longer did she have five senses, but only one—touch. All the others converged into total awareness of Cole and his possession of her.

She clung to his powerful frame, her fingers spread across his back, pulling him to her. Her slender legs held him tightly as the fervor that bound them heightened.

Rapture rippled, then surged through her like ocean waves. She wanted to give all of herself to him, to be complete with him. She could feel herself exploding in a sunburst of sensation.

Cole gasped. "Luv, now!" Shudders racked him, then a spasm gripped his body.

She and Cole were one, forged together in passion. Sheer bliss blossomed, assuaging her body's craving, satisfying her. Held in his strong arms, she was filled with joy, physically satiated, at peace with Cole. But as she lay beneath him, possessed by him, she was aware of an inexorable, invisible change.

In these intimate moments she had given him a part of herself and in return he had shown her a depth of pleasure she hadn't known existed.

He collapsed heavily on her and sanity began to return. Like a cat on a dark night, awareness of danger crept over her, silently, without warning.

Cole kissed her throat, then shifted to lay beside her. When he moved away, her skin felt cool. Perspiration bathed them both.

While he settled his arm behind her head and lay quietly, she gazed up at the dark leaves of a sycamore. A branch spread overhead and the moonlight through the leaves dappled their bodies.

She felt languorous, but also dazed, stunned by Cole's seduction. If the balloon had slammed to earth in a wheat field today instead of Cole's pool, she wondered if she would have felt any more stupefied than she did at the moment.

She was reluctant to move or rise or think. Cole reached out to smooth her hair away from her face. His fingers were gentle, soothing.

He leaned forward and kissed her lips, her cheek, her temple. "You're beautiful. You're wonderful, little green-eyed witch. You've charmed me."

She turned her head to study him. He lay with one dark leg thrown over hers, his tanned muscular right arm wrapped around her middle. His blue eyes were half-closed. It was a sin for a man to have lashes that curled so beautifully, she thought. Her glance moved to his lips, then shifted away quickly. His finger trailed along her chin to her ear.

Like a delayed bomb, reaction began to set in. A

tiny seed of worry sprouted and grew faster than Jack's beanstalk.

How could she have let him make love to her! How could she have succumbed to his seductive kisses after his somber warning, "I'm not the marrying kind." The past hour meant little to him!

In a husky voice he said, "You're quiet. What's going on behind those green eyes? Honey, that was magic. You've wound me around your little finger."

She listened in silence. What on earth had happened to her? She thought of his kisses, his intimate exploration of her, her wild responses to him, and felt waves of heat scald her.

A treacherous little voice reminded her how deliciously marvelous his lovemaking had been. She hadn't struggled with him. He hadn't used force.

While she fought a battle within herself, he continued caressing her, murmuring endearments that she paid no attention to.

He caught her chin and turned her to face him. "You're mighty quiet."

"I'm just thinking."

In the moonlit darkness he gazed at her solemnly, his blue eyes filled with concern. "Don't have regrets. That was a beginning between us. From now on, I won't rush you."

From now on? Did he think this would be a habit? But then, why wouldn't he think so, after her enthusiastic yielding?

"Honey, don't frown. It was too good for regrets."

She hated to admit just how good it had been. She was shocked by her actions. Never in her entire life had she acted so out of character. Never had she thrown aside everything, yielding with complete abandon to emotion and passion. Not until Cole Chandler.

She wasn't angry; she was aghast. How could she have allowed it?

"Marilee, luv. Would you please say something. Anything. Are you angry with me?"

She barely heard his question. She wanted to get up and pull on her clothes, get away from him. She wasn't accustomed to men. Even in the shadowy night, the thought of parading nude beneath Cole Chandler's watchful eyes sent shivers down her spine.

Softly, he said, "Yoo hoo, Marilee. Remember me?"

"How in hell could I forget you?"

"Uh oh. You are angry. Luv, that was—"

"I know, just marvelous."

He caught her firmly by the shoulders and looked at her intently. "It was unique, a beginning for us. I'm sorry if I rushed you. You caught me off guard . . ."

That was the hammer dropping on the percussion cap. Marilee's anger exploded. She sat up and swung her long legs off the chaise. "*I* caught *you* off guard!"

She stood up, hating the embarrassment of rising naked before him. Why did she have to be a redhead and so susceptible to blushes? Even in the dark, she knew he could see her pale flesh turning pink. Where had he thrown her clothes? She looked around frantically.

"Here, honey."

He sat up on the chaise and held a bit of lace out to her.

She felt sure she blushed from her ankles to her forehead as she snatched her white bikini panties from him. She balanced on one foot, stepping into the scanty lace as she glanced up at him. One arm casually on his knee, one long muscular leg stretching before him, he was watching her with a heavy-lidded gaze.

"You could have the grace to turn your head!" she snapped.

To her surprise he did. But she was glad for the chance to observe him without having to deal with his aggravating, seductive blue eyes.

His profile was strong, almost stern, and that, coupled with his hard, lean body gave the impression of a man who wouldn't lightly take no for an answer. But there was that devil that danced in his blue eyes. . . . His satiny skin glowed with vitality and health. Dark hair curled damply on the nape of his neck and for an instant she remembered what it had felt like to run her fingers through it.

Shaking her head as if to clear it, she pulled on her panties, then spotted his clothes lying on the ground. Picking up his slacks, she tossed them to the foot of the chaise.

Too late she realized the clothing would catch his attention. With a plop the slacks landed against his hip. He turned his gaze appraising her slowly, making another hot blush consume her.

She opened her mouth but before she could speak, he waved his hand. "Don't say it. I'll stop looking, but luv, you do have some dreadful hang-ups."

"I just have a shred of modesty!" He was beginning to aggravate her again. How could she have succumbed to him? She had collapsed like a house of cards in a windstorm. She found the sundress and slipped it on quickly, relishing the feel of the cool cotton sliding over her damp, heated skin.

Turning, she drew a sharp breath. Clad only in black hip-hugging briefs and holding his slacks, Cole stood facing her. Moonlight splashed over his hard shoulders, across his chest, highlighting the muscles of his magnificent body. He smiled.

In that moment she realized how far gone she was. She was in deeper trouble than she had guessed because his smile made her heart ping like a hot motor.

"Honey . . ." He started toward her again.

She put up her hand. "Stay right where you are, Cole. Don't come a step closer."

Four

"Marilee." His soft murmuring of her name weakened her knees, but it stiffened her resolve to get him out of her life quickly. She wasn't going to get involved in any sticky affair. She had no desire to experience again the pain she had felt when she'd lost her fiancé. She had a pleasant, productive life and Mr. Cole Chandler wasn't going to change it. Not at all, nosiree. If only her heart would quit thudding.

He continued to narrow the distance between them and when he reached her, he rested his hands on her shoulders. His voice became rougher, huskier, sliding over her raw nerves with a sensuousness that was another caress. "Maybe we were both vulnerable tonight." His hands slipped down her arms and around her waist. "How long, Marilee, since you've been loved like that."

Standing in his arms in the darkness, she couldn't answer because never, never had it been like that—so good, so devastating, beyond her control from the start.

As if he realized the reason for her silence, he said, "Let me rephrase my question. How long, period?"

She didn't want to admit to him, yet maybe he would understand better why she had fallen apart so swiftly, succumbed instantly to his seduction.

It was an effort to whisper simply, "Years."

"God! You might as well have taken vows and become a nun. I'm sorry. I'm sorry I rushed you."

He sounded contrite. Even so, she didn't want a temporary sexual relationship. And she didn't want her heart broken! Besides, there were too many demands from her teaching, her text books. She couldn't afford to get involved, even for a short time.

"I told you," she said, "I can't handle a casual affair. I'm too old for this sort of thing."

He laughed. "That's the most ridiculous statement I've ever heard!"

"Well, if I were twenty, or twenty-two or twenty-five, some age when life is still full of illusions and dreams, I might be interested, but not now."

He studied her and said softly, "Anyone who comes tumbling out of the sky in a balloon isn't too old for dreams."

"I am thirty years old and realistic. I don't like casual sex in spite of what just occurred. That happened this one time only and won't be repeated." She was pleased at the firmness in her voice.

The moonlight revealed his dancing blue eyes. "Thirty is a marvelous age," he said. "Especially to someone who's thirty-nine. And tonight wasn't casual."

His words stirred a warmth inside her that threatened to melt her resolve. At the same time it frightened her. She didn't want an affair to mess up her emotions and the easiest way to resist Cole was to get out of his life quickly. She was far too aware of his almost nude body. It disturbed her, tugged at her attention.

"Cole, will you dress?"

He smiled. "Sure thing." He stepped into the slacks and quickly fastened them. When he finished, she placed her hands on his muscular arms, liking despite herself the feel of his warm skin beneath her palms. "Let's forget tonight. My future is planned and there's no room in it for an affair. And I've been hurt too badly."

"How about a friendship? You're friends with that Jack."

"I don't think you and I can really settle for just friendship."

She started to step away, but his hands quickly clasped her about the waist.

"Why can't we settle for friendship?"

His blue eyes seemed to devour her and she struggled to avoid dropping her gaze to his mouth. She answered honestly, "There's too strong an attraction between us."

She warily held his gaze, watching as crinkles fanned out from the corners of his lids.

"That's good. At least you admit it."

She loosened his hands from her waist. "I have to get my clothes and I want to take Jack's balloon home."

Cole laughed. "You surely don't want it deposited on his doorstep. Give me the address where he keeps it."

She wondered if he meant what he said. He didn't seem the type to yield so quickly and easily. Shrugging mentally, she went inside to retrieve her clothing and wrote down Jack's address before rejoining Cole on the patio. He took her hand, walked her to a three-car garage, and seated her in a sleek, black Thunderbird.

He backed down the gravel drive and swung the car in a turn, sending a cloud of dust up behind them. As soon as they were headed away from the farmhouse, Cole's right hand cupped her shoulder.

"Come here."

She hesitated and he pulled her to him. "Come on. Stop debating something simple." He fitted her against his inviting body.

It wasn't simple. Every touch was a brand, a nerve-tingling searing of her flesh. His arm had dropped around her shoulder and his fingers were idly moving back and forth on her forearm.

While the car sped through the darkness, her mind raced as quickly over her promises to Cole. Deciding to let her friends give him an estimate on painting the house, she said, "When I paint, I work with two teachers, Ted Workman and Grant Smith. Ted's our choral director and Grant's the wrestling coach."

"There seem to be a lot of men in your life."

"They're just friends. We teach at the same school."

His fingers trailed lightly up and down her forearm while she looked across the dark fields. The familiar scent of his aftershave disturbed her senses, tugging at her memory of the last hour. "I should've been home typing tonight."

"Why?"

"I've started my second text. It's a follow-up to the first one."

"Who's your publisher?" When he talked she could feel the vibrations in his chest as she leaned against him.

"There's a company in Wichita. Century Press. I want to finish this second manuscript early in July."

"Why the rush? More houses to paint?"

She glanced up at his profile only inches away. His firm jaw was outlined darkly against the moon-lit night. "No, I have to meet a July thirteenth deadline because I'm going on a cruise." She didn't add she needed the money from her advance on the text to pay the remainder she owed on the cruise.

"Oh? Where'll you go?"

"St. Augustine, Barbados, St. Thomas. We're flying to Miami and leaving from there. I've never been on a ship, much less a cruise. I can't wait," she said, but for the first time, when she listed her itinerary, it didn't hold the magic it always had.

"We—meaning Ted and Grant?"

"Good heavens, no! Meaning Karen and Gina."

"Ahh, that's better."

"After your show in Kansas City, will you go back to Tulsa?" His fingers trailed higher, tickling the inside of her elbow. It had been miles back when he had pulled her beside him, yet the acute consciousness of his thigh pressed to hers, his long, hard body against hers hadn't diminished with time. Too clearly she recalled the feel of him when he had lain on top of her. She knew how muscled his bare legs were beneath the smooth fabric of his slacks. It was an increasing effort to follow what he said.

"I'll go long before July, about the middle of June."

Only four weeks from now! She sighed with relief, ignoring a threatening flicker of disappointment. Four weeks wasn't long. His aftershave was enticing, a barely noticeable fragrance. Four weeks. She hoped she'd get through the good night at her door.

He removed his arm from her shoulders and his

hand dropped to her knee. He pushed the cotton skirt aside to touch her bare skin. She couldn't have been more aware of his fingers if they had been tongues of flame hovering over her flesh, but Cole's conversation remained impersonal as he asked about her school, talked about wheat harvest and cattle. To have rejected his touch would have given it more importance than she was willing to admit. But the slow, feathery circles his fingers were drawing on the inside of her leg, just above her knee, were accelerating her pulse.

He turned down her wide street where the dark shadows of sycamore branches dappled the pavement. When he stopped in her drive and cut the engine, she stepped out of the car.

He met her at the walk and dropped his arm across her shoulders. As they walked to her door she mentally rehearsed three words. Good night, Cole. Say it quickly, go inside. Good night, Cole. How simple. Don't let him kiss you. . . . Her heart didn't get the message. It beat wildly as they climbed the porch steps, with Cole's boot heels scraping the boards. Somewhere behind the house two dogs barked.

"They don't recognize your car or know I'm here," Marilee explained.

"Your dogs?"

"Napoleon and Wellington."

He laughed. "Evidently they get along better than their namesakes did."

"They declared a truce. When they were pups they fought."

"Is this your house? Do you share it with one of those many sisters or your parents?"

She pulled her key ring from a pocket in her shorts. "It's mine. I'm the unmarried sister. My parents live a mile from here and two sisters live in Wichita."

Cole leaned an arm against the outside screen door, holding it closed, and turned her to face him. He toyed with the strap on her shoulder, smoothing it, brushing lightly against her skin, making her remember when he had so carefully lowered that strap.

His voice was deep and husky. "That's a mighty dark house. Would you like me to come in, make sure everything's safe?"

"Good try!"

"It might not be a bad idea, you know."

"I've been coming home alone a long time now. I'll let Napoleon and Wellington in and they'll check the house for intruders."

"I give up. Almost." His hand slid behind her neck and he pulled her forward slightly to meet his lowering head. His kiss reaffirmed their earlier passion.

He claimed her lips. He took her breath, her entire body. The ache she felt stirring in her loins, spreading hotly through her limbs, was more intense than before. His earlier lovemaking, instead of lessening her desire, of assuaging her needs, had only made her anguished body want more. He had awakened the hunger she thought was under control, diminished by long hours at work, by dedication to her career.

One of Cole's hands roamed down her back, sliding warmly against her bare flesh until he reached the thin cotton of her sundress. His fingers trailed lower, caressing the small of her back, following her spine, creating wild sparks of heat. When his fingers drifted over the slope of her buttocks, she began to struggle.

She caught his hard, bony wrist and pulled his hand away, twisting her head to free her lips from his. He buried his face in the cloud of red hair while he nuzzled her shoulder. "My auburn-haired witch!"

"Good night, Cole." Her voice was breathless.

Thick lashes lowered while he gazed at her through half-closed eyes. His voice was as uneven as hers. "Honey, today was very, very special."

"I think it would be better for us both to forget it."

"Now who's taking a relationship lightly—after your stern warning!"

"This isn't a relationship. It really isn't."

His brows narrowed over the bridge of his straight nose. "I hope, way down deep, you don't mean that."

Her heart speeded up. "You have me so confused I don't know what I'm doing—except telling you good night. I have to go."

He smiled and touched her cheek. "All right, but I'll smell your perfume all the way home, wish you were beside me, your knee close to mine. I'll hear your laughter, remember you tumbling out of the sky, dropping down into my pool, remember your kisses. . . ."

She clamped her jaws together and turned to unlock the door. In her haste, she dropped the key and it clattered on the porch. Cole picked it up and when she reached to take it, his fingers closed around hers, tugging lightly, pulling her hand to his mouth to kiss the inside of her wrist.

His tongue flicked against the heel of her palm, starting a fresh wave of reaction, a sweet longing, a remembrance of the night's intimacy.

Pulling free of his grasp, her fingers closed around the small metal key. "Some night soon you won't shut me out, Marilee," he said, his voice a low rumble. "Even now you can only close me out of your house, not out of your heart."

Without answering she unlocked the door and

stepped inside her house. She was trembling, thankful it was dark and he couldn't see her face. He didn't move, but stood across the threshold, his blue eyes piercing hers. "Good night," she whispered reluctantly and closed the door.

Standing without moving, she listened to his footsteps across the porch. Within seconds the car door slammed, then silence. She realized that he must be waiting to see a light come on. She flipped the switch, then hurried through the house, through familiar rooms filled with potted plants, her home which had suddenly lost its appeal. Thinking the dogs would help to alleviate her depression, she opened the back door of the screen porch and let them inside.

As the two silver afghans bounded into the house, she heard the motor of a car roar then fade into the night. She patted the dogs' slender heads, talking to them, watching their tails wag joyously in welcome. When she straightened, they followed her through the house but she forgot them instantly. She was thinking about Cole and the day It seemed years since morning. She glanced around her yellow kitchen with its potted plants. She loved the lush green plants for they gave her a feeling of something tropical in dry Kansas.

Switching off the lights, she walked through her small dining room with its round oak table and four chairs. By comparison to Cole's spacious farmhouse, her home was small, but it was comfortable. In her yellow bedroom her text lay on the corner of the dresser. She picked it up and held the thick blue book in her hands.

The Words You Read by M. L. O'Neil.

Cole Chandler threatened her career, her work, her peace, her existence. One weak moment wasn't the end of the world. She glanced at her reflection in her dresser mirror, staring at wide green eyes, the freckles across her nose, the auburn hair that curled softly over her shoulders. Yet all she could really see was her mind's image of thick-lashed laughing blue eyes, deep lines bracketing a full smile with flashing white teeth, dark brown locks of hair tumbling over a wide, intelligent forehead. He was so independent, accustomed to taking charge all the years he had been on his own and responsible for his sister, his work. Yet there had been moments when he'd sounded as if he needed her as badly as she did him. She shook her head. That kind of daydreaming could earn her a broken heart.

"Damn you, Cole!" she whispered. Wellington's tail thumped vigorously, arousing her from her reverie. She looked down at her dog and laughed.

"That's right. Damn Cole Chandler."

Both dogs wagged their tails and Marilee patted their heads before placing her book on the dresser. She bathed, determined to fight her memory of the day, but as she lathered a long, shapely leg, she recollected Cole's warm hands caressing her knee, her thigh. Shifting, she scrubbed vigorously, rushing through her bath before climbing into bed to find more agonizing memories taunting her. Forcing her thoughts to school, she contemplated the work she needed to do the following week.

Early the next morning, she called Ted Workman to ask him and Grant to look at Cole's house and give him an estimate, promising that whatever sum they decided to charge would be agreeable with her. She dressed, attended church, went by her parents' house for Sunday dinner, and didn't return home until almost dark.

She hadn't been there ten minutes when the phone rang. "Hello," she said into the receiver.

"Chicken."

Her heart jumped at the sound of Cole's deep voice and she laughed. "No," she said, "but I'm busy and I do have a little sense."

"I lost all mine yesterday when I was invaded by a gorgeous redhead."

"Yeah, sure," she answered lightly, but his words recalled their meeting, the image of Cole standing beside the pool.

"That was a dirty, rotten, low-down, sneaky trick to send two guys out here. I was showered, had on my Sunday best, all ready for a marvelous day. . . ."

"Cole, it's useless."

"That's what you think, honey. Your heartbeat relays a different message. Will you go to dinner with me tonight?"

"No, thanks. I have to get ready for school tomorrow."

"A short dinner?"

Don't argue with me, she thought. I'm far too vulnerable. Please don't push. "Sorry," she said. "Did you get an estimate?"

"Yep. You have a lot of male acquaintances. What do you mean you have no men in your life? Are those guys married?"

"I told you. Both are single and they're just good friends."

"Okay, if you say so. I know you have to eat dinner. You say no, but your voice changes each time."

She wanted to answer, 'Look what happened the last dinner we had!' Instead, she said, "No, thanks. I better go. . . ."

"Hey, wait. On the estimate for the house . . ."

Marilee gently replaced the receiver. If it made

him angry, it was just as well. Within seconds the phone rang again. She stared at it for a moment, then unplugged it from the wall.

Standing in the quiet living room, her voice sounded hollow and loud as she said, "Smart girl, Marilee. That was the right thing to do before you get hurt." She sighed. If only he didn't have so much appeal . . . She changed into jeans and a halter, fixed a cheese sandwich, and settled at her desk to grade papers.

Monday, when she was at school, she was able to forget Cole for whole minutes at a time. Two fans were humming at the front of her class room and every window was raised. Marilee smoothed a wisp of hair off the back of her neck, securing it again in the bun on top of her head. Even though she wore a white cotton blouse, a full blue skirt and canvas shoes, she was hot. During third period she gave a test and walked up and down the aisles to answer any questions and watch for cheating. The only sounds were her footsteps and the occasional shuffling of papers. She was standing at the back of the room beside Fred Lake's desk when the door opened and Cole entered, his boots making a clatter on the wooden floor.

Stunned, Marilee caught her breath as the moment froze in time. The sudden appearance of a tiger wouldn't have been more startling. Dressed in a pale gray western suit, Cole dominated the room, conveying a masculine air of authority as he walked leisurely across the front. He stopped by her desk, one hand resting casually on his hip.

Five

Thirty-three faces turned to look at her questioningly. She felt a flush consume her to the roots of her hair.

Cole grinned. His voice was strong and clear and thirty-three faces reversed directions when he asked, "I'm sorry to interrupt, but may I see you a moment, Miss O'Neil?"

Every eye returned to her. Cole had her at a disadvantage. If she refused, he would just wait. If that happened, not a student in the room would finish the test. She could feel curiosity swirling around her like warm bath water and knew it would be only seconds before someone started to giggle.

Along with apprehension came mounting fury. She was as angry with her office as she was with Cole. For the thousandth time she wished they wouldn't send visitors to a room without notice.

"Everybody go on with your test," she said sternly.

No one moved. All attention was on her as she started toward the front of the room.

Cole watched her walk up the aisle. It didn't matter where they met, what circumstances surrounded them, the impact of facing him was as great as ever. She was totally aware of every inch of her body as his blue eyes focused on her. She knew thirty-three pairs of ears waited for her words. The silence was total when she paused in front of Cole.

Whispering, even though her whisper could be heard throughout the room, she said, "I'll be happy to talk to you after class."

"No, I need to see you now," he answered in a normal tone of voice, his words carrying clearly through the quiet room.

"My students are taking a test and you're jeopardizing the results. Please go."

"I have an appointment in just a few minutes, so I can't wait to talk later." He paused then added bluntly, "Have dinner with me tonight."

Her worst fears were confirmed. Behind her someone snickered. Somebody else whispered, "Say yes, Miss O'Neil."

"Miss O'Neil's got a boyfriend!"

"Miss O'Neil's blushing!"

"You're ruining a test," she muttered between clenched teeth. Her anger bounced off him harmlessly. His blue eyes danced.

"Will you?"

"No, thank you, I have plans."

"She's going rollerskating with the class," someone said.

She prayed he would turn and leave. Smoke should be pouring out her ears from the heat in her cheeks.

"How about tomorrow night?"

"I have to grade papers." Go, get out!

73

Cole's blue eyes sparkled. He glanced over her shoulder. "Let's see a show of hands."

"Cole!" Laughter mixed with her aggravation. To her horror he blithely continued.

"How many think Miss O'Neil should grade papers tomorrow night?"

No hands went up as the class yelled, "No!"

"Hey, good! How many vote for a dinner date?"

Several boys whistled and all hands flew upward.

"Go on, Miss O'Neil! We'll skip a night of homework so you won't have to grade papers."

"We'll grade your papers."

Her cheeks burned with exasperation, and she had to fight an idiotic tendency to grin. "Cole, so help me!"

The moment she spoke, everyone immediately hushed.

Cole smiled. "It's unanimous. One dinner date instead of papers."

"After what you've done here . . ." she began.

"How about eight o'clock?"

"No! Now look, I have to grade papers."

"Go on, Miss O'Neil!"

"What's your name, mister?"

"What's his name, Miss O'Neil?"

"Miss O'Neil's boyfriend's cute!" someone in the front row whispered.

"How old do you think he is?" someone else whispered back.

She wondered if Cole would ever leave. She felt as if hours had passed since he entered the room. Laughter filled his eyes while he waited. She gazed into those blue depths and tried to hold on to her resistance.

"Go on, Miss O'Neil."

"Are you going to marry him?"

"Will all of you be quiet! For heaven's sake!"

"What's the answer?" Cole asked.

She had to get him out of her room! She relented. "If *you'll* go now, I'll go tomorrow night."

A cheer went up in the room that she knew could be heard all the way to the office. Whistles and applause added to the commotion until she waved her hand.

"This class better be quiet and finish that test or you'll finish it after school!"

Instantly a hush spread like a blanket. Cole suddenly grasped her hand in both of his, shaking it vigorously. His blue eyes danced as, in an exaggerated drawl, he said, "Miss O'Neil, thank you. You can't imagine how delighted I am."

She yanked her hand out of his. "I can't wait to tell you what I feel. There's the door."

Out of the corner of her eye she knew all attention was on them, but at least everyone was sitting quietly.

"I'm going," Cole said. With his long stride he headed for the door. As he opened it, he glanced over his shoulder at her and winked, waving at the class.

Inwardly, Marilee muttered oaths. He had broken the spell of quiet her threat had created. Students called to him, "Bye, come back!"

"Eat at Steak and Ale!"

Voices ceased abruptly when Marilee turned to glare at the students. The door closed quietly behind Cole and the class exploded with questions.

"Is he your boyfriend?"

"You going to get married, Miss O'Neil?"

"No. Now, quiet down. Go back to your tests. I want the questions answered and you'll get a grade, but we'll have to have another test tomorrow . . ."

Several students groaned. With a quelling look, Marilee continued, ". . . because of the interruption during this one. Now, everyone back to work. Bring your paper to the desk when you're finished."

Fighting to suppress laughter, she sat down behind her desk. One of the girls came forward to place her paper on the desk. "Are you going to marry him, Miss O'Neil?"

"Oh no, Lana," Marilee said without hesitation. She glanced at the clock. Ten minutes left in the third period. She couldn't wait until it ended.

Fourth period wasn't any better, but she wasn't surprised. Everyone in school must have heard about Cole's visit. She was besieged with questions until the final bell. Finally she sank back in her chair and stared at the empty desks. Thank goodness there were only four more days of school! If Cole had appeared in January and she had had a whole semester of questions and speculation, she didn't think she would have survived.

An hour later when she entered her house, the phone rang. She picked it up, knowing full well who was on the other end. Still, Cole's husky baritone voice unsettled her nerves.

"Hi, hon," he said cheerfully.

"You really did it today! Do you know what trouble you caused?"

"You brought it on yourself. You wouldn't talk to me on the phone."

"I've explained why. I'll never hear the end of rumors. You either don't know anything about teenagers or you're set on ruining my life. By sixth period someone asked me when our baby is due!"

"Gee whiz. What'd you say?"

"Dammit! I hear you laughing. You caused me a lot of extra work, not to mention mental stress."

"Just bear that in mind the next time you turn down a date with me."

"You don't look like the type to resort to coercion." It was becoming increasingly difficult to keep laughter out of her voice, to sound firm.

How easily she could picture his mischievous blue eyes.

"Thank you."

"Now, will you stay away from my classroom?"

"Maybe. What harm did it really do?"

"Oh, none. I just had three thousand questions to answer about my personal life. How old is he, how did we meet . . ."

"That must've been an interesting answer. What'd you say?"

"If I'd hinted at what really happened, do you know how many more questions I would've had? I said I met you at church."

"I'll be damned, you lied about church."

"Cole! Now I have to give another test."

"Hey. I'm sorry about that! Of course, you could've accepted my offer right away and I would've tiptoed out without a by-your-leave."

"That would be the day!" She suppressed a laugh. "I have to get ready now to go rollerskating."

"Eight o'clock tomorrow night, okay?"

Her heart beat faster at the thought despite herself. "I might back out. . . ." she said half seriously, as all her doubts began clamoring for attention.

"You do and I'll reappear in your classroom."

"Do you usually resort to blackmail to get dates?"

"If I say no, you'll think I'm conceited. If I say yes, you'll think I'm nuts."

"Right!" She laughed. "You are, I do, and don't come to class. I'll be ready at eight."

"That's more like it! Marilee . . ." he paused. When he spoke again his speech had slowed to a drawl, his voice had lowered to a husky, sensuous tone that came over the wire and stroked her nerves, set them afire. "Hon, I can't forget a moment, a kiss, a touch. . . ."

She tried to ignore the suddenly tightening coil

deep within her. "Cole, please don't," she whispered. "I'm having a hard enough time as it is."

"Then why fight what you feel? Oh, honey, my sweet auburn-haired witch. I want to hold you in my arms."

"Cole!"

"Yes, ma'am," he answered so contritely that the spell was broken and she laughed.

"I have to go rollerskating."

"Sure thing. See you tomorrow at eight."

Torn between excitement and wariness, Marilee brushed her hair and pinned it behind her head in a chignon. Satisfied that she was ready, she put the dogs outside and walked into the living room to wait for Cole. She knew she was playing with fire by going out to dinner with him, but surely nothing could happen in a public restaurant. But then there was the ride to the restaurant, the ride back, the good night kiss. . . .

The door bell rang promptly at eight and Marilee took one last look in the mirror, noting her shiny black high-heeled sandals, her sleeveless black dress, the faint touch of blush on her cheeks. Wondering if Cole would like how she looked, she picked up her purse and went to the door.

The impact of Cole was devastating. His smile faded as his blue eyes devoured her, drifting lazily down to her toes then returning to her face while she took in his appearance with a flickering glance, his dark jacket, the charcoal slacks, a white shirt open at his throat, revealing dark curls of hair. He stepped inside, closed the door behind him, and took her into his arms.

She resisted instantly. "Wait . . ."

"No way, luv," he murmured huskily while his arms tightened around her and crushed her to him. He kissed her hungrily and Marilee felt swamped in swirling emotion. Her need, her longing for him, surfaced. With it came fear, the reminder that she should use judgment, exercise caution. But beyond all that was the wild, inescapable thrill created by his kisses. His mouth on hers, his warm body, his one hand at the nape of her neck and one hard arm behind her back, built flames within her, making her cling to him. Finally, she broke away. While a giddy shakiness filled her, she smoothed her hair into place. He reached for her again, but she slipped past him to open the door.

"This way to safety, to dinner, to peace of mind."

He stood in the hallway, one hand on his hip, his smoldering eyes challenging her. "Do you really think so?" he drawled.

He was like a heady drug, churning her senses into a delirious high. "Cole . . ."

Dropping his hand to his side, he smiled and ushered her outside, closing the door behind them. Standing only inches away from her, he said, "There's only one thing I'm hungry for. A luscious, red-headed witch."

Each word added kindling to the bonfire blazing within her, but she ignored them as best she could. "It's a good thing my door locked when you shut it and I have the key."

He smiled. "Come on. I'll feed you, hungry woman."

Aware that her appetite had changed as drastically as his, she descended the porch steps with him to where the black Thunderbird was parked by the curb. As they drove toward the expressway, she asked, "Have you had any more planes? Any trouble with rustlers?"

"Yes and no. Yes, the plane was spotted last

night about dusk and no, we haven't had rustlers yet."

They entered the expressway, heading south. Cole adjusted the rearview mirror, then dropped his hand to her shoulder to pull her close.

"Come here," he murmured. "Don't you know this is where you belong?"

She scooted close to him while he wrapped his arm around her. She hated to admit how marvelous it felt beside him, as if she did belong there. His aftershave was enticing, a delectable masculine, woodsy scent. Through their layers of clothing she felt the warmth of his body.

He changed lanes smoothly, speeding up as they whipped through the evening traffic along the flat highway. She noticed him studying the rearview mirror, alternately glancing from the mirror to the road.

"Wait a minute." He raised his arm to put both hands on the wheel.

She frowned as she studied his profile, the firm jaw, taut mouth, cold blue eyes. "What's wrong?" she asked.

His words were clipped. "We're being followed."

Six

Her blood seemed to turn to ice. "Followed! Why on earth would . . ."

She knew before the sentence was complete. Cole was a wealthy businessman with several lucrative ventures. Kidnappers might profit handsomely from abducting him. Her heart began beating faster and it was an effort to keep from turning around to peer at the traffic behind them. She slid back to her side of the car.

"What'll you do?"

A muscle worked in his jaw as he abruptly changed lanes, cutting narrowly across traffic to whip onto an exit. He swore while behind them brakes squealed and horns honked.

"They almost wrecked their car," he said, "but they made it off the expressway too. They aren't going to be easy to lose."

The Thunderbird shot down the narrow exit ramp to an access road running parallel to the highway. At a four-way stop Cole slammed on his brakes, then accelerated to spurt across the intersection. His body was tense; his hands gripped the wheel tightly. Marilee squeezed her eyes shut as another car halted abruptly to avoid hitting them broadside.

"It's the green Buick behind us," he said tersely.

She glanced back at the busy intersection to see a dark green dented Buick and its two male occupants. One look at the bushy blond hair of the driver and Marilee gasped.

"It's Fred!"

Cole's head whipped around. "Fred?"

Shaking with relief, she let out her breath as Cole swept up a ramp and reentered the expressway.

"It's Fred Lake and Scott Hogart. They're my pupils."

"My God! I just aged a year."

"Now you know how it feels."

"Why're they following us?"

"Why do you think? After your appearance at school there are one hundred and fifty teenagers from all of my classes who have nothing but time on their hands and enormous curiosity."

Laughing, he shifted in his seat, relaxing his shoulders as he slowed down.

"It's not funny," she said, crossing her arms over her chest. "I don't care to be watched like a monkey in the zoo."

"A monkey? Oh, not a monkey. A long-legged, classy cheetah maybe, but not a monkey," he drawled softly, sending a delicious shiver down her spine.

He put his arm around her shoulders and pulled her close again. Smoothing the soft black crepe of her dress over her knees, she said, "It's a good thing school lets out this week. Are they still behind us?"

"Yep."

"You know they saw you put your arm around me and they can see how closely we're sitting. Tomorrow will be pure torture. I'll have to be an ogre to keep everything under control."

"My sweet ogre." He kissed her temple and settled back against the seat. "I'd lose them, but I'm afraid they'll take some risks and get hurt. They had a close call back there when they cut across the highway."

"Drive a little slower, please. I wouldn't want anyone hurt."

"They must like you or they wouldn't be interested in what you do."

"We get along all right, but they're going to wonder why I'm so mean the last week of school. They'll follow us to dinner."

"That's okay. They won't eat with us."

"I know, but it still makes me feel like something in a zoo."

He squeezed her and laughed. "Forget them. Maybe I should help you forget . . ." His hand slipped across her collarbone and down the front of her black dress.

She caught his blunt fingers and moved them back to her arm quickly. "The last thing I need is for them to pull up beside us and see your hand all over me."

"Give them something to liven their day."

"Oh, brother. Not at my expense. You've given them enough as it is!" He exited off the expressway, then drove down a wide street lined with elms. Tires crunched on gravel as they turned into the driveway of Luciano's, one of Wichita's most elegant restaurants. Marilee gave a silent sigh of relief. It was expensive and required reservations and dress other than blue jeans. She hadn't been convinced that they might not have her students at the next table while they ate, but now she relaxed.

When she stepped out of the Thunderbird, she saw the green Buick whip past on the street.

"There they go," Cole said. "Now you can forget them." He took her arm and escorted her up a canopied walk lined with pots of pink geraniums."

A white-jacketed waiter seated them in a secluded alcove. Adding to the elegance of the thick red carpet, crystal chandeliers, and white linen tablecloths, a bouquet of rosebuds and tulips sat in the center of the table. In the distance a young man softly played a piano and a few feet away from their table was a window where mock orange and spirea bushes bloomed outside.

Marilee sat across from Cole and each time their eyes met, sparks were set off. Her attention focused on him alone, shutting out awareness of their surroundings. She barely noticed when the wine list was placed in front of them and was surprised when Cole asked, "What kind do you like best?"

"I'll trust your judgment."

"Good!" He winked at her, making her pulse jump with anticipation. "Keep that attitude. How about champagne?"

Her brows raised with surprise, but she simply said, "Fine."

Cole gave the order and the waiter returned shortly with a bottle in a bucket of ice. As soon as Cole approved the champagne, the waiter poured two glasses.

Once they were alone, Cole gazed at her across the centerpiece of flowers. His dark hair was feathered away from his forehead, but one unruly curl twisted over his temple. His blue eyes had darkened to a smoldering indigo. Beneath his scorching study, she felt her heart beat faster. He lifted his glass, extending it to her. "Here's to faulty balloons."

"And soft, cushy swimming pools," she answered breathlessly.

"What happened to your voice?"

"I don't know."

"Liar." A lazy smile played across his features.

Hastily, she clinked her glass against his, raising it to drink. She sipped the golden, bubbling liquid and lowered her glass. "This is nice." Nice, exciting, dangerous . . .

"I think so too."

He settled back in his chair and glanced around. Suddenly his dark brows flew together. "Dammit," he said softly.

"What's wrong?"

Cole stared out the window. "I'd swear I saw a face at that window just now."

She stared at the spirea and mock orange bushes. "Someone may be gardening."

"No, he ducked down when I looked."

"Are you sure? Why would . . . Oh, no! Fred and Scott."

Cole swore again and Marilee laughed. "What's wrong? What was it you said? 'It'll give them something to liven their day.' "

"I don't want two pimply peeping Toms ruining my romantic dinner with you!"

She laughed. "They're outside. They can't do much. But I don't think I'll drink the rest of my champagne."

"Why not?"

"Have you forgotten your teen years?"

"Thank God, yes."

"If I drink a whole glass of champagne, tomorrow the rumor will be all over school that I'm an alcoholic."

"That's ridiculous."

"It isn't. I'll guarantee you it—" Movement caught her eye and she turned. Bushy red hair ducked out of sight below the window and a spirea bush shook frantically.

"That was Horse Jones!"

"Horse?"

"His real name is Valentine Jones. He asked me to call him by his nickname. He's close friends with Fred and Scott." While she talked she watched the window.

"Well, hell! We're not going to go through dinner this way." He scanned the dining room. "This place is a bunch of damn windows."

"You're getting very touchy. You didn't think much about it when I said I felt I was on display in a zoo."

His blue gaze returned to her. "Don't rub it in. I could go out there and run them off."

"I don't know how you raised a younger sister," she said, shaking her head with mock wonder. "You don't know one thing about teenagers. They'd lead you a merry chase." She looked at the window in time to catch dark hair ducking out of sight. "There's a bunch out there. That looked like Terry Hankins."

"Let's go to the farm and I'll cook steaks again."

"Your ignorance is appalling."

"What now?" He sounded annoyed.

"They'd follow us unless you drove so recklessly that they might wreck their car."

"Well, dammit! What're you laughing at?"

"You run several successful enterprises, but these kids have you buffaloed!"

"Watch out, woman. You're pushing your luck," he threatened in mocking tones.

She grinned, glancing at the window to see two heads drop out of sight. "There went Fred and Horse. You've really brought yourself some trouble with your little visit to school."

"My, you sound smug."

She wrinkled her nose at him. "Revenge is sweet. You'll know better next time than to walk into my classroom and stir up everyone."

He rose to his feet, walked a few steps, and surveyed the restaurant. While he stood still, a few customers turned to observe him. She couldn't suppress a laugh at the scowl on his face. He was so damned handsome, standing there with one hand resting negligently on his hip. Her gaze ran the length of his body, down his long legs before rising to meet his eyes as he returned.

"I don't know why it's so funny to you now."

"If some of your employees could see you!"

He glowered, rubbing his forehead thoughtfully. "They're ruining our evening. There isn't a table in this place that isn't in sight of a window."

He sat in silence for so long, she asked, "What's going through your mind?"

"I'm thinking about other restaurants. A place with no windows."

"If it allows jeans and isn't too expensive, they'll eat at tables around us."

His scowl deepened. "I could call the waiter to chase them away."

"They'd just come back when he went inside."

His blue eyes flashed. "You know so much about those monsters. Do you have any suggestions? Can't you step outside and threaten them like you did in class?"

She shook her head. "Sorry. If I headed for the door they'd shoo like flies. When I returned to my seat, they'd be right back. Relax, Cole. I do this every day over lunch."

"Dammit! I wanted a secluded, romantic dinner with a sexy, beautiful woman. What do I get? A bunch of half-baked adolescents leering through the window at us every few minutes!" He finished his champagne in a gulp.

He had called her beautiful and sexy! She felt like purring. "Don't drink too much or they'll spread the rumor that I'm dating an alcoholic," she teased.

"Look, Marilee . . ."

"I guess it's not important with school out this week." She looked at the window and caught Horse with his nose against the glass. She waved. He ducked out of sight, spirea stems jiggled, sending showers of white petals flying, then five faces rose into sight and grinned at her.

"Smile, Cole, we have an audience." She waved while Cole turned to the window.

"Dammit!"

"You better smile."

"I'd like to clobber every one of them!"

The five boys grinned and waved.

"They're harmless and they're outside," she said calmly.

"Oh, yeah. And isn't this romantic! Waving to a bunch of grinning goons won't set the right mood."

She gazed at him innocently. "Mood for what?"

"Stop laughing, Marilee! I'll be right back."

He shoved away his chair and crossed to the window. Marilee watched with curiosity and amusement. She couldn't see anything except Cole's back and his hand gesturing and pointing toward the door. In a moment he turned to go outside.

The boys waved again and left, shaking more blooms off the spirea and mock orange. She picked up her glass and drank, laughing softly. Since it appeared their entire evening was going to be chaperoned, she certainly didn't have to worry about Cole's getting too close. But he had been so endearing as he tried to figure out what to do with five pesky teenage boys. . . . She looked up to see Cole walking toward the table, looking pleased.

He crossed the restaurant in his long, easy stride, his jacket open, swinging loosely. Breathing became difficult for Marilee. Her heart was hammering by the time he sat down. He refilled both of their glasses, raised his in a toast, and smiled into her eyes, sending her pulse into orbit.

"Here's to money. I paid the little devils off."

"Oh no!"

He lowered his glass a fraction while his eyes narrowed. "Now what?"

She shrugged, clinking her glass against his. "I don't want to worry you. You looked so happy when you came back," she said sweetly, enjoying herself. When she was with Cole everything seemed sunshine and roses, so good. She knew his anger was on the surface, that a stronger emotion tugged at both of them, and she felt safe enough with her self-appointed chaperones to revel in that emotion. "We'll wait and see if your method was successful."

"I don't like the sound of that. Why won't it be successful? They promised they'd go away, although it cost me a bundle. I wanted to knock their heads together. I don't know how you keep your hands off them."

Sweetness dripped from her voice. "Now you know why I wasn't happy to see you in my classroom."

"But it did get me a date. Next time don't hang up on me."

"Mmmmm."

"Now, why won't it work to pay them off? Don't be evasive."

"You sound like a hungry bear."

He took a deep breath and expelled it slowly. "Marilee . . ." His voice was threateningly soft.

"Let's forget them." She glanced out the window. "Your idea to pay them was grand!" she said cheerfully. "They're gone, so we'll enjoy our dinner."

He stared at her suspiciously for long moments before looking out the window again. Finally he settled back in his chair and relaxed.

"All right. Let's start the evening over."

The waiter appeared with menus. Cole recommended the specialty of the house, fresh salmon flown in from the Pacific Northwest, and they ordered it cold, poached, along with boiled new potatoes, and salad with a lemon dressing.

They were halfway through the delectable meal when Marilee glanced out the window. "Cole, I hate to tell you this, but there's another face at the window."

His eyes widened as he turned to look. He swore softly. "I paid them! They promised me . . ."

"They did just what they promised."

His head snapped around and he glared at her with angry blue eyes. She laughed and explained. "This is a different bunch. If you pay them, they'll go and call someone else to come. They've hit a jackpot."

"Well, I'll be damned! That's why you groaned when I told you I'd paid them. I might as well have taken you to the school cafeteria to eat!"

"This is a smidgen nicer." She turned to catch Jerry Klaus and George Hamilton grinning at her. Dusk had set in, but outside lights illuminated the white blossoms and revealed the boys clearly.

"Don't wave," Cole said, obviously still annoyed. "You'll encourage them."

She laughed again. "It doesn't matter. They're here to collect."

"Well, they're in for a disappointment. Am I

going to have to go through this every time I take you out?"

"Oh, no. Only until the novelty wears off. Of course, with school over this week and time on their hands . . ." She spoke lightly, but the words 'every time I take you out' lit a glow inside her that she recognized as extremely volatile.

He picked up his glass of champagne. "Why do I get the feeling that you're laughing at me? That you could stop them, but you're enjoying yourself?"

She struggled to keep her features solemn, lost the battle, and smiled. "I'm not laughing at you and I really can't do anything about them. But you did pique their curiosity."

"Yeah."

"It might help a little if we ignored them, as if we'd forgotten about them."

"That'll be a pleasure."

"You know I don't prefer this to the alternative," she added softly. "To eating with your full attention."

He set down his glass, his eyes deepening with intensity. The moment became taut while charges bounced between them.

"This is pure agony." He placed his hand on the table. "With our audience out there, is it permissible to hold your hand?"

She gave it a second's thought, then shook her head. "No. I don't want to hear about it tomorrow. I'll get a blow-by-blow description anyway."

"This is worse than having dinner with a girl's parents." He moved his hand away and picked up his fork. "Who're the two guys who paint with you?"

"Ted and Grant? I teach with them." She thought about Grant, a handsome man with thick blond hair, a cleft in his chin, velvet brown eyes, and broad shoulders. They had dated briefly, but there wasn't any spark between them. His kisses were nice and forgettable. And it must have been mutual. They remained friends, but the dates ended.

"Grant's the blond?"

She nodded. "He's the wrestling coach and teaches history in the room next to mine. Ted Workman and I met at Wichita University when we took a course together."

"That guy, the coach. Do you date him?"

"Sometimes." She felt a little flare of satisfaction.

"Lately?"

She stared directly into his blue eyes. "No."

Crinkles fanned from the corners of those eyes. "I don't think you date the other one either."

"No, I don't. Ted's nice. We're friends. Because of his red hair a lot of people think he's my brother."

"You hardly look alike. The only resemblance is that he has red hair as long as yours. He looks as if he hasn't had a square meal in his life. That six-four frame is all bones, whereas your frame is covered with the most luscious curves. . . ."

"Oh, really?"

His gaze whisked away the black crepe, and heated her blood. In a low voice he said, "Come on. I'm ready for a little privacy."

He signaled for the waiter and paid the bill, then pushed back his chair and walked around the table to her. His fingers drifted across her bare neck as he reached down to pull back her chair. When she rose, she looked up into smoldering blue eyes that conveyed an unmistakable message. Unable to move, to break the magic spell between them, she drew a sharp breath.

His voice dropped to a husky note. "Right now, you feel the same thing I do."

She did. She ran her finger along his jacket lapel, unable to keep her hands off him.

Cole caught his breath. "Let's go before I do something to make you the school's choice topic."

As they walked through the dining room, Marilee was aware of each brush of her bare arm against his soft jacket sleeve, of his height and broad shoulders.

When they stepped outside a cool breeze enveloped them. Night had fallen but the floodlights in the tall elms made the front drive as light as day. The Thunderbird was brought to the door and they climbed inside. As Cole whipped out of the drive, he looked into the rearview mirror and swore.

She twisted to see an old Ford full of kids.

"Marilee, I want to lose them."

"Oh, please don't. They'll give chase and if they had a wreck, if anything happened, I'd never get over it. Most of them haven't been driving very long."

His jaw had a stubborn thrust. The feathered locks of wavy hair had blown into unruly curls, giving him a reckless appearance. "I haven't spent an evening like this since I was fifteen years old!"

"Puts a little crimp in your style, eh?"

His arm swept out, pulling her to him in a tight hug. "If you don't stop laughing at me, I'll wreak my revenge!"

"Mmmm. Sounds interesting!"

He chuckled and pressed her against his hard length so that the warmth of his body penetrated her thin layers of clothing. Excitement streaked through her, caused by his vitality, his presence. After a minute she asked, "Are they still behind us?"

"Can you forget about them?"

"Hardly."

"Yeah, they're there."

"Cole, may I make a suggestion?"

"Sure."

"Don't race away, but lose them before you go home. They don't know who you are, but if they find out where you live . . ."

He groaned. "I think it would be easier to have terrorists or the Feds after me. At least I could give them a chase."

She laughed, relaxing, and lay her head against his shoulder. In spite of the harassment, the evening had been fun. Just being with Cole was exciting, regardless of what they did. She moved a fraction to gaze up at his jaw, running her finger over his rough skin, across the tiny bristles.

Without taking his eyes from the road, he turned to catch her finger lightly with his teeth. His tongue touched her fingertip, sending a shower of sparks through her. She pulled her hand away. "Your attention might drift."

"It did. I'd like to pull over and take you in my arms. But I know I can't with the goon squad on our heels." He took a deep breath. "Luv, I have to leave town tomorrow. I'll be back next week. I had other plans for tonight."

His last words did something to her heart. "Sorry, I think." She wondered where he was going, what he would do. The thought of Cole's absence left a cold, leaden feeling. From that first kiss he had been special. With each passing second in his company, he was becoming more important to her. He filled many of her needs. She wondered about his needs. His broad shoulders looked as if he could carry responsibility without help. Yet there was that defensive note in his voice when he talked about his parents. There were all the fences he had erected around his home. She wondered if he had barriers around his heart. Was his gruff announcement that he wouldn't marry, a fence he put up to keep her at a distance? Was his implacability limited to marriage or did it include any degree of commitment?

While she mulled over these thoughts, Cole slowed the car and stopped in front of her house. When the motor died, they could hear the high chirping of crickets through the open window. Cole peeled off his coat and draped it over the seat between them. "It's been fun," Marilee said. "Thank you."

Slipping his arm around her waist, he smiled. "There's no car behind us."

She held him away. "There doesn't have to be. I imagine my bushes are crawling with bodies, all ears for our every word."

"Well, damn!" He surveyed the darkened yard, the flowering shrubbery.

"Cole, it was fun, but I can't kiss you at the door in front of them. We'll say good night right here and now." She sighed with true regret. "I'm sorry, but I have to maintain my authority, my reputation. I can't be the object of their jokes."

"Marilee, this is a nightmare."

She leaned forward to kiss him lightly. Instantly, his arm tightened with the inflexibility of an iron band, crushing her against his hard chest. Through the open window they heard a giggle.

Marilee moved away, whispering, "Sorry. I better go."

Cole escorted her to the door. They stood in the darkness on the porch while he unlocked the door. Before he opened it, she grasped his strong fingers and squeezed them.

"Good night and thanks for a fun evening."

"Talk about maintaining a reputation. This is a first for me!" he murmured. When she laughed, his teeth nipped lightly at her neck. "Just you wait!" he whispered, sending a shiver rippling in her.

"Bye."

A chorus of voices suddenly shattered the quiet. "Kiss her good night!"

Someone whistled. Marilee had an instant of stunned surprise as she peered into the darkness. She saw the pale oval of a face in parted lilac fronds. Bushes waggled and the face disappeared. Aggravated, she said, "See?"

Cole placed his hand beside her head, barring her from the door. His other arm slipped around her waist. In a normal speaking voice that carried across the yard he drawled, "I think that's the best idea they've had all night."

Her heart thudded against her ribs. She reached behind her back to try to push the door open. "Oh, Cole, no . . ."

"Kiss her, mister!"

"Cole, don't you give in to them! I'll never hear the end—"

He stopped her protest, crushing her in his arms while his lips took hers in no uncertain manner.

His mouth opened hers, possessing her in a kiss that curled her toes, that caused the roar in her ears to blank out the whistles and cheers. How long was he going to kiss her, she wondered. It was her last rational thought. Her mind was lost to sensation; resistance left her body. She melted against his hardness, wrapping her arms around his neck. Dimly she heard cheers, shouts, but the sounds blended, fading into nothing.

On and on went his deliberate exploring, his plundering kiss. The air became rarefied, her breathing difficult.

Finally he relented. Applause and raucous shouts filled the air while she stood dazed in Cole's arms.

With his arm around her waist, he turned and bowed deeply. "Now, you guys, how about some privacy!" he called.

"Oh, my Lord," Marilee whispered while there was more applause and a few ribald suggestions. "So help me, Cole! Do you know what you've done to my life now?"

Opening the door for her, he grinned. "Wasn't it worth it?"

In spite of her aggravation and the knowledge that tomorrow she would pay for his kiss, she smiled. She stepped inside, turning to block him. "Now, go while they're still around to see you leave!"

Chuckling, he said, "Night, hon."

She locked the door and switched on the lights. Laughter shook her as she thought about Cole and their chaperones. She thought again about how much fun it was to be in his company. Yet if she had any sense, if she wanted to avoid a real heartbreak—because she was sure Cole had all the potential to give her one—she wouldn't see him again except professionally. "Good thoughts, Marilee," she whispered to the empty house as she heard the Thunderbird roar away. "That's the same thing you said last time."

During the rest of the week, she took the teasing at school good-naturedly. Friday finally came and she turned in her grades and books, cleaned her classroom, and closed it for summer. With Cole out of town and unable to bother her, she got a good deal of work done on her book—except when she was daydreaming about Cole.

On the Tuesday after Memorial Day, she stepped out of Ted's truck and picked up a ladder to start work on the Chandler farmhouse.

"I'll tell him we're here," Grant offered, pushing scrapers into his pockets.

Ted lifted down another ladder. "I'll start at the front." His paint-spattered coveralls hung loosely on his freckled bony frame as he shouldered the ladder and sauntered around the side of the house.

Within minutes Grant reappeared. "Chandler's not here," he said to Marilee. "There's a woman working in the kitchen. I told her we're the painters." He picked up the ladder and Marilee followed him to the back of the house. While Grant began working at ground level, Marilee climbed up the ladder and started scraping old paint, loosening it before they applied the primer. It was a miserably hot day, and her thoughts were divided between speculation about the possibility of heat stroke and memories of the last time she was at this house. Those memories unfortunately only made her hotter.

During mid-morning a man dressed in jeans, a plaid shirt, and boots strolled around the corner of the house, pushing his wide-brimmed hat to the back of his head. "Miss O'Neil?" he called up to her.

"Yes?"

"I'm Charley Williams. Mr. Chandler's out of town today. He asked me to tell you his nephew Henry won't be here until tomorrow."

"Fine. Thanks."

Charley turned away and Marilee continued automatically scraping the house, wondering if Cole had forgotten her. She had been trying not to notice the orange-cushioned chaise on the patio and the inviting blue swimming pool because of memories they stirred of Cole. She missed him. Far more than she wanted to admit.

By the time she reached home at the end of the day, she was hot and exhausted and heading for the shower when the phone rang. Yanking up the receiver, she heard Jack Wilson's cheery hello.

"Did you get your balloon, Jack?" she asked.

"Sure did. Thanks, Marilee. It couldn't have worked out better."

He sounded too happy over a smashed balloon and a suspicion struck her. "Did Cole return your balloon?"

"No. He told me to buy a new one and send him the bill. And not to spare the expense."

"Jack, he was supposed to return your wrecked balloon."

"Well, he can keep it or you can. I'm perfectly happy with my new one."

"Don't send him the bill." At that moment she could have cheerfully wrung Cole Chandler's neck for giving Jack encouragement to purchase a new balloon. She braced herself and asked, "What did it cost?"

Her knees almost buckled at the figure. "That's enough for a DC-9!"

"It's a bit high," Jack admitted without shame. "You must've really made a hit with him. What'd you do to get him to pay that much?"

Rage burned inside Marilee as she bit her lip in furious silence. Along with her anger was a sickening lurch as she calculated swiftly what it would take to earn the amount of the new balloon. It was difficult to grind out her next words.

"Send me the bill."

"Oh, forget it, Marilee. Chandler can afford it and he wants to. It's too late anyway. He already has the bill."

"Jack, I can't turn in an insurance claim if he pays it."

"Don't yell at me. The whole thing's your fault." His voice deepened. "I've got a beauty of a balloon. A real beauty."

"Don't you think you should've purchased something in line with what you owned before? That's almost twice as much as your old one! It's an astronomical figure." Why had she ever been friendly with such a jerk?

"You know he can afford any kind of balloon he wants. Is he in love with you?"

"No."

"He's sure willing to hand over a lot of money for you."

"Dammit!"

"Want to go out tonight? I'll treat."

She held the receiver away from her and glared at it. When she pulled it back to speak, each word was clipped and precise. "Jack, I'll pay him for the balloon. You're costing me and I can't afford it. I didn't wreck an expensive one and you know it!"

"Chandler offered to pay. I've sent him the bill. That's all there is to it. I'll see you around."

The phone clicked. She lowered the receiver, muttering darkly about Jack's principles.

She pulled out her checkbook and wrote out a check for Cole. As large as it was, it didn't cover a third of the cost of the new balloon. And it would take her within fifty dollars of her savings, but she was determined that Cole wouldn't pay.

For a moment she toyed with the idea of canceling her cruise. It had lost the magic it had held for so long. It meant separation from Cole. She brushed away the worry, knowing she couldn't cancel. She had already paid for half of it and she would lose a hefty portion of her money. She had planned and saved for two years to go on this cruise with Karen and Gina. It would ruin their plans if she backed out now. She stared at the check. Why would Cole spend so much on her? Something warm unfolded inside her, a feeling that was so good when she thought of her moments with Cole. And with her memories came a longing that only he could meet.

She called her insurance company, but the agent was out so she left her number and pushed away worry about the expensive balloon.

The next day, while she was standing high on the ladder with the hot Kansas sun beating down on her, the black Thunderbird whipped into the garage and she heard a car door slam. Nothing changed outwardly, but inside everything quickened, her awareness of her surroundings heightened. She leaned against the house and continued to slide her scraper calmly along the boards, chipping off the white paint. When the patio gate banged open she slowly swiveled her head and looked down.

Seven

Cole stood below, one fist on his hip, a suitcase in his other hand, dark glasses hiding his eyes. His white shirt was open at the throat, his tie loosened, and his shirt sleeves turned back. His pale blue suit coat was draped over his shoulder. The lurch of her heart told Marilee how effectively she had her feelings under control, despite her casual demeanor.

"Hi," she said.

"I had to go to Tulsa. How's the scraping?"

"It's fine. Coming right along."

"Want a drink of ice water?"

"No, thanks. I have a thermos."

He smiled and went inside. She climbed down, moved her ladder a few inches to the left, climbed back up, and continued scraping. Why did everything seem different now that he was back? She was conscious of her appearance—her faded cutoffs, ratty sandals, blue shirt and floppy straw hat—of the hot sun, the gentle breeze. All of her senses were sharpened now that Cole was back. Forcing her attention back to the scraping, she moved the ladder again and continued to work as the sun climbed higher and the summer heat intensified.

She had scraped to the edge of a window when it suddenly opened and Cole appeared. His wet hair was plastered to his head and his coppery shoulders were bare. Only inches away, he grinned at her. "Hi again, beautiful."

Glancing at his bare shoulders, she remembered too much about him—his long tanned body, muscular legs, hard thighs. She scrutinized the board she was scraping. "Careful," she said, "I may flick specks of old paint in your eyes."

"I'll take that chance. Want to swim?"

"Sorry, I'm working."

"I asked your partners. They want to."

Startled, she paused. "They do?"

He nodded. "And by the way, thanks, but I tore up your check."

She stared at him. "You can't."

"I already have."

"If you do, there's only one reason. Do you know what that makes me," she whispered, teasingly, "if you pay for sex with me?"

"You know better than that! I paid for the balloon because the guy was giving you a hard time, I can afford it, and I wanted to."

She turned back to her scraping.

"Jack asked me what I did to get you to pay."

"Jack's a real peach."

"I know. I don't see him anymore." She stopped scraping and looked at him seriously. "You can't buy his new balloon, Cole. Let me turn in an insurance claim. I'm licensed and insured. It'll be covered."

"I told him to buy whatever he wanted," Cole said stubbornly, "so I brought some of the expense on myself." He smiled coaxingly. "It's too hot to argue about it right now. Stop scraping and come swim."

"I don't have a suit."

The corners of his mouth tugged higher. "I suspected you might use that excuse. I brought you one."

"You're joking!"

He rose and she saw the ends of a white towel and the top of his brown legs. She shifted her weight as she watched him cross the room to a suitcase on the bed. He opened it and rummaged through it, dropping clothes on the floor. The sight of his almost naked body weakened Marilee's knees and she tightened her hold on the ladder.

He snatched up something triumphantly and returned to the window. He leaned out and presented some scraps of brightly colored material.

"See. Here it is."

"How did . . ."

He grinned. "Come on. Knock off for a while. It'll be lunch time soon. Swim and eat, then you can go back to work."

"It may not fit."

"But it might. Give it a try. Here, I can lift you in through the window."

He stretched out his tanned arms and his hands closed on her waist.

"I'll fall," she said, tightening her grip on the ladder again as electric shocks ran through her at his touch. "I'll come in through the kitchen."

"This is easier." She started to climb down, but he tugged her toward him. "Throw your leg over the sill. I won't drop you."

Holding her hat on her head, she did as he instructed and climbed safely through the window.

As soon as she was inside, his arms closed around her and pulled her close.

She chuckled. "This feels familiar. You, me, and a towel."

"Do you know how much I've missed you?"

"You couldn't have," she said, resisting the urge to melt against him. How good his words sounded! How much she hoped he meant what he said. "Where's the swimsuit?"

He smiled at her obvious change of subject and released her. "Right here. I'll help." He started unbuttoning her blouse.

"Oh, no!" she gasped, but it was an effort to move out of his reach. Something started churning inside, a motor that sent her pulse thumping.

His hands dropped. "I forgot all your hang-ups!" he teased as he handed her the suit. "You know where you can change and just take a towel out of the bathroom."

She started across the room, but paused at the door. "I meant it about the balloon. You're not to pay."

"That's between Jack Wilson and me and has nothing to do with you anymore. Forget it."

"I can't. It makes me feel like a . . . a floozy."

"Oh, yeah?" He started toward her, his blue eyes dancing. "If that's the case, you'll do whatever I want for a price, how about . . ."

"Stuff it! You know what I mean."

He chuckled. "Go change and let's swim."

"All right, but this isn't the end of the matter."

She crossed the hall to the pink bedroom, closing the door behind her. The overhead ceiling fan revolved slowly, stirring a delicious breeze. Tossing away her straw hat, she stripped off her clothes and quickly showered in the adjoining bathroom. After she'd dried off she looked skeptically at the two tiny pieces of red, green, yellow, and blue material she was supposed to wear to swim.

Who had sold him that suit? She wished she had her simple one-piece black one.

Sighing, she picked up the halter and tied it on. It was too big and she wondered what size he thought she was until she pulled on the bikini bottom, which was too small.

Tugging it into place, she gazed at her reflection in the mirror while she tried to tie the halter more securely around her. Too big on top and too small on the bottom. At least his concept of her was flattering.

Too much bare midriff showed. She twisted and made a face at the gaudy stripes stretched tightly across her bottom. The suit barely covered the necessary regions and she didn't want to parade herself in front of the three men in it. But the thought of swimming in cool water was too inviting to pass up. She crossed the hall and rapped on Cole's open door.

When no one answered, she looked inside. "Cole?"

The room was empty and she walked over to the window. From there she could see the pool. Cole was standing at its edge, Grant was poised on the end of the divingboard, and Ted's red hair glistened in the pool.

Looking back at Cole she felt that familiar twist the sight of him could stir. From his gorgeous blue eyes, down his lean body and long, muscular legs, the man was too handsome! And too much fun.

"Watch it, O'Neil," she muttered and turned to his closet. Inside a row of shirts hung together, organized and neat. She pulled down a long-sleeved blue cotton dress shirt and slipping into it, stepped in front of the full-length mirror.

It hung to mid-thigh, the cuffs draped over her wrists, and it covered everything she wanted covered. Satisfied, she left to join the men.

The moment she stepped through the gate and closed it behind her, she suspected Cole had been waiting for her. He sat at the deep end of the pool, his fingers curled over the edge, legs dangling in the water. Ted and Grant were both swimming.

She saw Cole's quick appraisal of her as she walked toward a chair. The setting was very familiar—the chaise Cole had been sun-bathing on on that fateful day, the blue cordless phone on a small table beside it.

She put her towel down carefully, avoiding looking at Cole. She knew he was waiting for her to take off his shirt. A movement caught her attention and she turned to find him standing only a few feet away, his arms folded over his chest. It was just as much effort to keep her gaze from straying from his face to the rest of his tantalizing body as it had been during their first meeting.

"How does the suit fit?" he asked.

She waggled her fingers. "So-so."

They stared at each other in silence.

"You're blushing," Cole remarked after a minute.

"Well, you're embarrassing me. Don't study me that way."

His blue eyes danced with glee. "I can't wait! I've been dreaming about this moment since I handed over the money for the suit."

"I may go back and dress."

He laughed. "Come on, take off my shirt."

"All right, but stop staring." She shrugged out of his shirt, ignoring his low whistle.

"It fits, doesn't it?"

"A little tight over the nether regions . . ." She walked to the pool, and stepped off the edge, dropping straight into the cold, refreshing water.

Within seconds she found Cole swimming beside her, his long strokes matching hers as she swam the length of the pool. After eight laps, as they faced each other momentarily, he grinned. "How long can you keep up this pace?"

"Until I'm exhausted. I love to swim."

His grin widened and he swam alongside her as they continued the laps. When her muscles began to ache, she slowed, struggling to finish the lap until finally, inches away from the diving board, she caught the edge of the pool and stopped, panting for breath.

Cole treaded water beside her. "I thought maybe you hoped to drown me."

He didn't sound winded at all. She gulped for air. "You didn't have to swim with me."

"I wanted to. That's why I bought the suit."

"I want to pay for it."

"It's a gift."

"Thank you."

"Stay and have dinner. I'll take you home."

"I can't." Be positive, she reminded herself. Firm. "I'm racing to get my text done this summer. I have to make my July deadline. School starts again in August, so I can't be late getting this finished. I hope to have this new text out to follow my first one, go a step farther."

He swam closer, his leg brushing hers while he rested both hands on the edge of the pool, on either side of her. "You must have quite a bit of faith in your method."

She hardly heard what he said. "I've seen the results of it," she answered, more breathless than before. "I think everyone should be able to read. If they don't like it or don't care to—that's each person's decision, but they should have that choice. You're getting too close."

"If we were alone, I'd be closer," he said in a low drawl that started shivers up and down her spine.

Grant splashed noisily nearby. "This is fantastic!" he shouted.

"Good," Cole answered over his shoulder. "Feel free to use the pool anytime you're here."

"Thanks!"

Grant ducked beneath the surface and swam away. Cole's attention returned to Marilee.

"One evening shouldn't put a kink in your schedule," he said in a low, seductive voice.

"Thanks, no." She was determined not to give in again. "I have to meet my deadline or I won't get to go on the cruise and I won't have my second book ready for the fall term a year from now." She couldn't think of anything with him inches away, with his leg brushing between hers. "It's imperative . . . umm, you're too close."

"What's imperative?"

She couldn't remember. "Where's your nephew?"

"Henry'll be here this afternoon." A warm note entered his voice. "He's something else. He attracts dirt like a magnet does metal filings. If he gives you a hard time, let me know."

"He won't."

"He's had some problems at home. Besides moving so much, his mother has had two divorces. Henry's father lives in Wyoming."

"I'm sorry."

"Want to see who can touch bottom first?"

"It might be safer than what we're doing now."

"Oh? We're not doing anything."

"Let's touch the bottom of the pool." She took a deep breath and sank. Cole went with her, his arms closing around her while he pulled her close for one moment. The touch of his almost nude body, wet and warm against hers, exploded longing in Marilee.

Wriggling free, she shot to the surface. Cole's head broke water a few feet away. "Chicken. You didn't touch."

"Oh, yes, I did." And her heart still pounded from the contact with him.

Ted climbed out of the pool and called to them, "I'm eating lunch now. Anyone want to join me?"

"Yes," Marilee said thankfully. "Soon it'll be time to get back to scraping." Anything to fight the wild longing for Cole.

Cole grinned at her. "Don't you know all work and no play made Jack a dull boy?"

"But not Marilee. I thrive on it. That's my life." She slipped below the surface, shutting out his retort as she swam past him under water to the side of the pool. Climbing out, she ignored all three men while she hurried to the chair and pulled on Cole's shirt.

Ted munched a sandwich, and pointed to a brown sack on the table. "There's your lunch, Marilee. I brought all the bags from the car."

"Thanks."

Grant toweled off and moved to sit in the shade on the concrete beside them, pulling his black metal lunchbox in front of him.

Cole came up swiftly at the end of the pool, water splashing off his brown body. For an instant, Marilee felt a lurch in the middle of her stomach. Cole's hard body glistened in the sunlight, muscles rippling, the tight black trunks molding his trim hips.

She dropped her gaze to her brown paper sack, not even looking up when Cole offered them cold drinks. Grant and Ted asked for beer, and she asked for a soda. Cole went into the house and when he returned, dressed in jeans, he was carrying a tray with the cans of cold drinks, a large plate of deviled eggs, a mound of potato chips, and warm chocolate brownies.

He placed the tray on a blue wrought-iron table within reach of everyone, then dropped down to sit cross-legged beside Marilee. The men chatted while Marilee ate her peanut butter and jelly sandwich, trying to ignore the light pressure of Cole's knee against hers.

When he was through eating, Grant rose and stretched. His golden body was fit and strong from wrestling. Glancing at him, Marilee wondered again why she could study him without a tremor, yet a mere glimpse of the lean hard torso beside her sent her pulse into high gear.

Quickly finishing her sandwich, she left to change her clothes. She hung her damp suit over the rack in the bathroom and dressed again in her cut-offs and work shirt. She stepped out of the bathroom and into the bedroom, then halted abruptly when she saw Cole. He was leaning negligently against the doorjamb, still dressed only in jeans.

"How long have you been here?"

He smiled and walked into the room, closing the door behind him.

"Oh, no!" she whispered, but she didn't—couldn't—back away.

"Oh, yes." His arms slid around her waist. "One kiss won't ruin your day. Come here."

He pulled her to him. His skin smelled faintly of chlorine and water, his breath had the slightest tinge of spearmint. With the first pressure of his lips on hers, Marilee's banked desire burst into flame, and she pulled his head closer.

Heated, moist, a reminder of the ecstasy they'd found before, his mouth teased hers, brushing her lips, stirring sensations that built like boiling storm clouds. Emotions churned within her as his tongue met hers, seeking response, giving pleasure. Each stroke, each bit of pleasure added to the tension, the charged atmosphere, the threatening deluge of passion. The tip of his tongue lazed over the roof of her mouth, causing wild sensations.

Holding tightly to her last shred of common sense, she reluctantly stepped out of his embrace, her hands resting lightly on his forearms. "That's enough, Cole."

"Is it really, Marilee?"

"Yes. When I look at you all I can see is a threat. Don't pressure me. Grant and Ted are waiting."

His blue eyes were smoldering. "Why don't you stop fighting what you feel? Enjoy life, enjoy your body. You're struggling against something marvelous and natural."

His words stung. She held back so little; he held back so much. "What are *you* fighting, Cole? You give your body willingly, but what about your heart? Do you allow the emotion in your heart to surface?"

He blanched with such a look of pain she wished she could take back the words. "I learned a long time ago how to take care of myself, Marilee," he answered flatly. The barriers were up. She could almost hear them click into place as a shuttered look hid his feelings. He turned for the door. "Henry will be here shortly."

When the door closed behind him, she felt a painful twist inside. His words had hurt and she had hurt him. She couldn't give her body free rein with Cole without her heart going along for the ride—heading straight for calamity. He was so self-sufficient, yet just now his independence had looked painfully lonely.

Determined not to dwell on Cole, she went back outside and climbed up her ladder again. She reminded herself it was just as well. Only three weeks until he left the farm. Three weeks and he would walk out of her life forever. She didn't want to be his summer fling, a fleeting affair, easily forgotten. She was too vulnerable. She knew it would take very little more contact for her to be head over heels in love with the man and he wasn't "the marrying kind."

Reaching the top of the ladder, she looked into the open window. She could see Cole's king-size oak bed, a dark blue quilted spread, dark blue carpet, and the clothes he had dropped on the floor.

Determined to avoid another encounter, she climbed down and moved her ladder away from his window. Scraping vigorously, it was only minutes before she felt as if someone had moved the thermostat to two hundred degrees. The heat was unbearable. There wasn't a hint of breeze and the sun was beating down relentlessly.

The back door thumped shut and she looked down to see Cole cross the patio without a glance in her direction.

Her heart ached as she watched his straight back, the long stride. He wore a broad-brimmed black hat, jeans, a pale blue cotton shirt. He disappeared into the garage. Within a short time she heard a car start then roar away down the drive. Trying to banish nagging demons, she worked furiously.

After awhile, she noticed Ted standing on the ground watching her.

"If you scrape any faster," he observed, "your arm'll drop off."

"I want to finish this job."

"Mr. Chandler's a nice guy, Marilee."

"Why're you telling me that?"

"He seems interested. I didn't mean to pry."

"You're not." She mopped her brow. "Now I know how a boiled lobster must feel."

Ted nodded. "If we don't get rain, it'll get worse." He started walking away, then added, "I think Mr. Chandler's back." As Ted strolled around the corner of the house, Marilee could hear the car again. She tried to continue scraping, but all of herself was concentrating on Cole. She heard the back door open and shut and looked down.

"There you are," Cole called up to her. "Henry's here."

"I'll be right down." Just keep calm, she told herself, although she was acutely aware that Cole was watching as she climbed down the ladder.

"I'll put away my things," she said when she reached the ground, keeping her back to Cole.

A whoop sounded around the corner and a small boy ran into view. He was a miniature of Cole with laughing blue eyes, thick brown lashes, and dark brown curly hair.

"He looks just like you!" Marilee exclaimed.

"Thanks," Cole said dryly. "Henry!"

The eight-year-old boy stopped to stare openly at Marilee. His freckled face was smudged with dirt, his short-sleeved beige cotton shirt was half in and half out of his jeans, and his torn sneakers were scuffed and untied.

"Believe it or not, this was a clean, presentable boy when I picked him up," Cole said. "Miss O'Neil, this is Henry Baxter. Henry, this is your teacher, Miss O'Neil."

" 'Lo."

Marilee smiled. "Hi, Henry. I have to put things away and then we'll start."

"Well, I'll leave you two alone." Cole's gaze rested warmly on Marilee. "If you need anything, call me."

"Thanks."

Henry studied some pebbles in his hand, not looking up as his uncle strolled away.

"Want to help me?" Marilee asked the boy.

Blue eyes met hers. "Yeah, sure."

She held out the scrapers and a wire brush. "You carry these and I'll get the ladder.

Henry's short, grimy fingers closed around the handles and he dawdled along behind her to the truck. But by the time she had everything loaded, Henry was laughing, telling her about his new puppy, Frisky.

After Marilee retrieved her blue denim workbag from the truck, they moved to the shaded patio. As soon as they sat down Jada appeared with two tall glasses of lemonade and a plate of cookies. Finally, when they were alone, Marilee listened to Henry read a few pages from a storybook.

His brow puckered and he pronounced the words slowly. When a few words didn't make sense, she realized Henry was guessing if he didn't recognize the word.

Stopping him, she reached into her bag and pulled out a deck of cards made from thin cardboard, each painted with letters.

"Do you know how to play rummy, Henry?"

"Yep. Think so." He pushed curls away from his face and wriggled in his chair.

"I made these cards. See each one has a letter painted on it or a combination of letters." She continued explaining how to play the game, using phonics to sound out the letters on the card.

Within a few minutes Henry sat forward, the tip of his tongue showing at the corner of his mouth as he studied his cards. Gradually, he caught on to the game and began to play with more ease. After a time they changed to another game involving phonics.

Finally Marilee glanced at her watch. "It's time

to quit. Let's total the last score." She added quickly while Henry leaned against her back and watched. His thin body was a light pressure against her shoulder and he smelled faintly of rubber and unwashed gym shoes.

"Hey, you won!" she said. "One hundred and three points to my ninety-eight."

He grinned. "We gonna play tomorrow?"

"Sure will."

He touched a red curl on her neck. "You smell good."

"Thank you."

"You Uncle Cole's new girl friend?"

"Henry!" Cole pushed the back screen door open and stepped outside, his black boots showing beneath frayed jeans. "Time's up, Henry. Miss O'Neil has to go. Her friends are loading their equipment on the truck."

Marilee watched in silence as Cole walked to within a few feet of them and hooked his hands in his broad leather belt.

"Can I ride Blaze now, Uncle Cole?" Henry asked.

"Sure. I'll be there in a minute."

Henry started across the patio, but Cole's voice stopped him. "Henry!"

The boy jerked his head in Marilee's direction. "Oh. Bye, Miss O'Neil."

"Bye, Henry."

He slammed the patio gate shut as she gathered up her belongings. It opened immediately and Grant glanced at them. "Pardon me . . ."

Interpreting his look, Marilee said, "You're not interrupting anything. I'll be right there."

He smiled. "Good. So long, Mr. Chandler."

Cole waved casually, but his blue eyes were solemn as he gazed at her.

"Henry's bright," she said.

"You know kids."

"Yes, I do." She paused. "Totally honest."

Cole didn't misunderstand. "I haven't led a monk's life, Marilee."

She laughed despite herself. "Don't be defensive. It isn't that big a deal," she lied.

He crossed over to her and tilted her chin up, his blue eyes probing hers. The slight pressure of his fingertips on her jaw made her pulse thump. She pulled back and bent to pick up her bag before Cole saw more in her eyes than he should. "Henry responds beautifully," she said, forcing herself to speak calmly. "I think all he needs is one-on-one attention."

"You sound so sure." Cole's chest heaved with a long sigh. "He's had that before—one person working with him."

"Give me two weeks and you'll see an improvement."

"You may be too hasty in your promise."

"I've done this before, remember?"

Suddenly his features changed. Crinkles fanned from the corners of his eyes. "Two weeks, huh? Fine! I've always liked someone who's positive."

She ignored the warm feeling generated by his praise. "Well, they're waiting. Bye, Cole."

He reached the gate ahead of her, his brown hand holding it open. His voice was soft as he said, "Bye, Marilee."

Something hurt. Suddenly Cole looked as vulnerable to heartache as she. Confused by his somber expression and her own feelings, she hurried to the truck and squeezed in between the two men. She rode home lost in thought about the day, Cole's kisses, his appealing body, the tempting offer for dinner, the words they had exchanged.

*   *   *

The next two days passed quickly. Marilee, Grant, and Ted would work throughout the morning, then Cole would appear around noon and invite them to swim. Marilee brought her one-piece black racing suit with her and Cole's blue eyes had danced the first time he saw her in it, but he made no comment about her preference in swim wear. He also seemed to be purposely keeping his distance from her, as though he had sensed her reluctance on Tuesday and was willing to give her the space she needed. Although Marilee appreciated his sensitivity, she couldn't hide from herself her longing to be in Cole's arms again.

But, she told herself as she started scraping the side of the house the following Friday, it was for the best if both she and Cole let the passion that had erupted between them die a quiet death. He'd be leaving in two weeks, she'd be going on her cruise. . . . She tried to quell the pain that rose at the thought of their imminent separation.

She worked without stopping, cursing the heat wave which showed no signs of slacking. At noon she changed into her suit and headed for the pool.

When she reached it, Cole was the only person in sight. He was treading water and his blue eyes appraised her with a smoldering glance that made her draw a sharp breath.

"Come on in," he said, his voice suggestive. "The water's just right." He twisted to float on his back and the sunlight glistened on his bronze shoulders and the dark mat of hair curling wetly on his chest. She avoided studying the narrow black swim trunks. Water splashed over his long brown legs as he bobbed up and down with the waves caused by his moving hands.

She dropped her towel in a chair and jumped into the water, relishing its soothing coolness.

The thermometer had already climbed to an even one hundred and she had been miserable scraping on the sunny side of the house. As she surfaced she heard a car motor rumble to life and fade away.

Cole swam over to her, tossing his wet hair away from his face. His hands caught her about the waist. "Hi, witch."

Aware of the occasional brush of his legs while he treaded water, of his hands holding her, her pulse drummed rapidly as she answered, "Hi."

"How's your text coming?"

"Right now I just want to forget it."

"I'll see what I can do to make you think of something else."

She laughed and ducked under water, then surfaced to swim laps up and down the pool.

While she swam, she knew Cole was watching her with a burning scrutiny. Where were Ted and Grant? They always beat her to the pool. She swam another lap and looked around.

Eight

As Marilee swam to the side of the pool, suspicion suddenly struck her. "Where are Ted and Grant?" she asked.

Cole extended his hand, reaching down to lift her out. She relished the faint breeze as she stepped onto the concrete—and the feel of Cole's hands lingering on her waist. His blue eyes were direct as he answered her question. "I sent them home."

"What about Henry?"

Cole shrugged. "I gave him the day off too."

"Cole . . ." She felt a glow spread throughout her body. She ignored reason, danger. She was alone with Cole—what she wanted more than anything else.

He held up his hand. "You work too hard, Marilee. Take an afternoon off." Motioning her to sit down at the table set for two, he said, "I told Grant and Ted I'd drive you home."

"It might've been nice of you to ask first."

He grinned. "And risk another rejection. No, thanks. Sit down, honey."

She toweled off, and then he sank in the other chair. On the blue wrought-iron table between them were tall glasses of iced tea, two plates, a bowl of potato chips, a plate of sandwiches, and a platter of chocolate-chip cookies.

"Where's my sacklunch?"

"On its way back to Wichita. Ted'll probably eat it. I think the man has hollow arms and legs."

She laughed. "I'll have to admit this is more appealing."

Cole took a swallow of iced tea. "Sandy's going to take off work soon so she can meet you. You're sure you're not corrupting Henry's morals with those comics you give him?"

"Be thankful he's reading them and enjoying them. Besides, they're harmless. You haven't read any or you wouldn't accuse me of evil."

He grinned. "No, I haven't read them."

"Pick one up and look at the vocabulary in it."

"I'll do that."

She accepted a sandwich of tuna salad on wheat bread. While they ate, conversation was casual, but Cole's eyes were conveying their own message. After a long lunch, Cole brought out two rafts and they floated lazily in the pool.

Marilee watched the brilliant white thunderheads overhead as their shapes drifted and changed against the blue sky.

"This is perfect, Cole," she said with a sigh. She didn't add, "With you."

She closed her eyes. Her fingers trailed in the water and the bobbing of the raft was soothing. She forced her mind to stay blank while she listened to the clear whistle of a redbird and the buzzing drone of cicadas.

Cole's voice was a deep rumble close at hand. "I told you, you work too hard."

She opened her eyes to find him propped on an elbow, lying on his side on his raft.

An all too familiar longing to touch him filled her as she gazed at his hard bronzed torso only inches away and the thick brown hair that curled over his neck.

Pulling herself under control, she closed her eyes again and paddled slightly away from Cole. He didn't speak again and, hypnotized by the silence, the heat, the gentle motions of her raft, she fell asleep. She awoke later, disoriented. The sky above was clear and the raft was motionless against the edge of the pool. Cole was sitting on the concrete, his legs dangling in the water, studying her.

She rubbed the sleep out of her eyes. "I'm sorry. I fell asleep."

He slipped into the water. "Don't apologize. I'm glad you did. Been burning the midnight oil?"

"I was up until two a.m. working on my textbook last night."

"Don't you know there's another way to live?" He pushed the raft away from the wall and swam beside her.

"I know, but I have to finish on time." She closed her eyes again against the bright sun. "I don't want to miss that cruise. I've planned and saved for it a long time. The thought of it carried me through two long dreary winters of grading papers."

Suddenly cold water dropped on her midriff and she yelped and sat up. Cole tipped the raft and she rolled off.

Water closed over her head, waking her fully. She reached out and grasped his legs and yanked him under. As soon as his head dropped below the surface, she let go and kicked away to escape.

Like a steel clamp, an arm snagged her about the waist, pulling her down. She struggled, trying to remember to keep her mouth closed.

His arms dropped away suddenly and she burst through to the surface, gulping air.

"You'll drown me!" she sputtered, laughing.

They were inches apart. His hand rested on her shoulder and one of her legs brushed against him as she treaded water. The laughter faded from his blue eyes to be replaced by an expression of smoldering, sensual desire.

"It's been almost two weeks, honey," he said in a low tone.

"What has?" she asked, knowing exactly what it was.

His voice mocked her as he softly repeated her question. " 'What has?' You know damn well."

Her pulse jumped as his arms encircled her while his lips possessed hers in a hard, demanding kiss that opened her mouth fully to his.

They floated together, held up by the movement of Cole's legs. They drifted to the shallow end and when they could touch bottom, he pulled her against him, hip to hip, her breasts crushed against his solid chest. Their skimpy suits were the only barrier between their water-slick bodies. She could feel his arousal, just as she knew he felt her nipples thrust against the matted hair on his chest.

She wrapped her arms around his neck, momentarily overwhelmed by his kiss, returning it hungrily while her heart pumped violently.

It was so good. His arms, his kisses so right, perfect. Why did he have such an effect on her? She wanted Cole Chandler as she had never wanted any man in her life. But did she want him enough to pay the price?

He leaned back slightly and smiled at her. "Hold your breath."

His arm tightened and he yanked her under the water with him, pushing her away as she struggled.

She had closed her mouth just in time, startled at the abrupt change. The cold water washed away the lethargy induced by his kisses.

She swam away from him, surfacing in time to see him hit the water with the palm of his hand, sending it spraying over her.

"Want to race?" she challenged.

"Sure."

"To the steps and back. Go!"

She had a slight lead, but she suspected he would catch up quickly. As she splashed across the pool as fast as possible, she wondered why he had stopped kissing her. She pulled her arms through the water, fighting to stay ahead, using all her energy to overcome the aching need created by his kisses.

He won by a yard. Tossing hair away from his face, he grinned. "My, you're competitive."

"Naturally."

"I thought women were supposed to graciously allow the male to beat them in competitions."

"What do you think I just did?"

His arm snaked out swiftly, but she ducked out of reach. "Why are you grousing? You won."

"Yeah, after swimming like hell. Sure you haven't been in the Olympics?"

"Very sure. I take aerobic dancing during the winter and I jog a little."

"I'll bet you do! Speaking of dancing—there's a little rodeo and barn dance at Arkansas City tonight. Would you like to go?"

"I'll have to get something to wear."

"No, you won't. It's a hot night, wear your cut-offs."

"And my old shirt?"

"If it makes you feel better, I'll wear my worst. Wear one of Sandy's dresses. They seem to fit you."

"I have so many pages I set myself to type each day. This will throw me off schedule."

"Don't you allow extra time?"

"I used it up long ago."

"One evening, a few hours, won't be the end of your schedule."

"Against my better judgment, all right."

"Your eagerness might inflate my ego," he said dryly. "If you had to choose between me or that blond Adonis you work with, it'd be different. Instead, the question is whether you want my charming company or want to type all evening?"

She laughed. "You poor thing!"

He swam toward her with a wicked gleam in his eye and she splashed away, swimming quickly toward the opposite end. He caught her halfway and dunked her, holding her under while she struggled.

Desperately, she reached out to tickle him and he released her. She surfaced, gasping for air.

He came up facing her and draped his arm about her shoulder. Drops of water glittered on his thick eyelashes and his dark hair was matted wetly on his forehead.

His blue eyes bore into her, working their magic with her pulse. "Ready for a cold drink?"

"Yes." Her voice was a croak, but he didn't seem to notice. "I think my skin is shriveling."

"Let me see . . ."

"Cole!" She swam away and climbed out of the pool. She was aware of his blue gaze on her as she picked up her towel. He swiftly followed her and wrapped a white towel around his middle.

The sight of him as he had been that first afternoon brought back a flood of stormy memories. She turned away and sat down in one of the chairs.

In spite of the hungry look in Cole's blue eyes, he spent the rest of the day doing nothing more arousing than teasing her, flirting mildly, and touching her casually, yet continually.

They sat in the shade by the pool and drank several glasses of iced tea while they talked about the world, Kansas, politics, Henry, art, music. They swam again, talked again, and ate Jada's chocolate-chip cookies.

All afternoon Marilee wondered whether Cole was purposely trying to tantalize her or if he was as unaware of what he was doing as he appeared. Each brush of their hands, every mild contact, fell like a spark, a tiny ember. One alone could easily be extinguished, but the continual onslaught smoldered until it became a conflagration that singed and threatened to envelop her in its blaze. She wanted to pull his arms around her waist, to be kissed until she forgot her torment.

Finally he rose and stretched. Marilee instantly lowered her eyes from the sight of his rippling muscles, remembering how she had placidly watched Grant stand in almost the same place and do the same thing. The brief glimpse of Cole though made her long desperately to be in his embrace again, recalling exactly how that lean, hard frame felt.

She rose swiftly. "I think I'll change."

He draped his arm around her. "Take your time. I'll throw something on for dinner and we'll go after we eat."

They walked to the house and their bare legs brushed, thigh against thigh, hip against hip.

When they entered the kitchen, it was quiet and empty. "Where's Jada?" she asked.

"I gave her the night off. I'll cook something simple. Okay?"

Contrary to his casual hold on her, his blue eyes were starting to smolder with unmistakable desire again. She nodded. "I'll be quick."

She went upstairs without hesitation, realizing how accustomed she had grown to moving through his house. She glanced into his bedroom, seeing his bed neatly made with the dark spread covering it. She closed her own door and leaned against it, knowing she should be home typing, doing anything but spending hour after hour with that seductive male.

What she was doing was exactly like placing a bowl of cream in a room with a hungry cat and wondering what the outcome would be, yet she couldn't turn down the challenge of the evening, demand to go home, sit alone, and work.

She stared at herself in the mirror. The ends of her still damp hair were matted together and short wispy strands curled in ringlets around her face. Without makeup, the freckles on her nose showed clearly.

"You're asking for trouble," she told her image seriously.

"But he's so damned appealing," she whispered back.

Heading for the shower, she thought about the afternoon and her yearning deepened. Casually, slowly, with each tantalizing contact, he had teased and heightened her desire for him. She lathered her red hair and scrubbed it thoroughly, trying to stop thinking about Cole.

One glance at her raggedy cut-offs sent her to the closet to search through Sandy's things. Finally she settled on another sundress, a dark blue cotton one with white piping. She slipped her feet into the large sandals and brushed her hair. She found a thin white ribbon in her purse and tied her hair in a cool pony tail.

Downstairs a cloud of smoke wafted into the hall from the kitchen and the tempting odor of frying meat assailed her. Dressed in jeans and a blue western shirt, Cole stood at the stove, enveloped in smoke.

"Should I call the fire department?" she asked dryly.

Cole turned. "Hey! You look great!"

"Something's burning."

"Yeah, me. Come here."

"Cole, that skillet . . . The kitchen will catch on fire."

"Who cares?" His arms closed about her while he held a spatula away from her. She relented momentarily, returning a kiss that coaxed a need for more.

"Cole, something's on fire!"

"Hmmm?" He strolled back to the stove, turned off the burner, and placed a lid over the skillet to smother the flames.

"Dinner'll be well done."

"It smells delicious anyway. Can I help?"

He waved his hands. "Everything's ready. French fries, minute steaks—a mite crispy—tossed salad and green peas, the only vegetable besides potatoes worth eating."

They ate on the patio, washed the dishes hastily, and left for Arkansas City.

It was cool and quiet in the car, the air conditioner making it pleasant. Marilee gazed at the fields spreading away on either side of the highway. Bright yellow acres of sunflowers alternated with golden wheat and with stretches of green dotted with grazing brown and white Hereford cattle.

"How's Bonny Charles?" she asked.

"Still safe and sound."

Which was more than she could say for herself, she thought. Each moment with Cole forged a tighter chain on her emotions. For a second she thought about the stack of typing waiting at home, her text which was so important. Then she glanced at Cole's profile, his thick, curly lashes that made his blue eyes so sexy, and forgot her typing completely.

They entered Arkansas City, driving down the cobbled stretch of highway through the center of town, passing beneath spreading branches of tall elm trees. They went to the rodeo first, sitting on makeshift wooden bleachers as they watched the cowboys burst out of the chute for bronc riding. It was warm and dusty, and the odors of horses and leather mingled with the tangy smell of popcorn. But even as she cheered with the rest of the crowd, Marilee paid scant attention to the riding. She was more interested in Cole, sitting so tantalizingly close to her.

When the rodeo was over, they drove to a huge red barn where the dance was. Cole introduced her to a few of his friends who were there, then led her to the dance floor. Fiddle music filled the air, mixing with laughter and shouts and the sound of feet stomping in the dust.

She and Cole danced constantly, whirling across the floor, advancing and retreating in time to the lively music. Marilee laughed continually with pleasure, delighting in Cole's lithe movements, his easy grace and warm smile.

They drank cold cider and danced some more until finally he put his arm around her shoulders and led her toward the exit. "Ready to go?" he asked, slightly winded.

She nodded and they strolled out into the darkness to their car. As they drove home it was cool enough to leave the windows down, letting night air rush in.

Marilee snuggled against Cole without complaint, but when he headed west out of town, she pushed away. "You're going the wrong direction," she said.

"Let's have a moonlight swim."

"No!"

He slowed to pull off the highway, then cut the engine. With a rustle of movement he took her in his arms, leaning his hard body over her, bending her head back against his arm as he kissed her.

His lips opened hers insistently, his driving hunger taking her breath away. His uncontrolled desire was apparent and in a primitive reaction, she arched against him. An aching need for him swept her arms around his neck as if he were her last hold on life. No matter the dangers to her heart, she wanted him desperately with all her being. The surge of emotion between them as they kissed banished the barriers between them.

Breathing heavily, hardly able to articulate, Cole said, "Come home with me, honey."

It was impossible to say no to him when he held her in his arms. Every inch of her strained toward him. Her breath exhaled in a soft, "Yes."

As he slid away and started the car, Marilee realized how deep a commitment she had made to him. That first evening when she had succumbed she had been able to argue away her guilt, promising herself it wouldn't happen again. Tonight was different. She had consented freely to go home with him, even though her rational mind was telling her not to.

Cole's fingers curled around hers and he squeezed her hand. "Stop worrying. Everything's too marvelous to worry."

"It is right now," she answered, wondering how long the magic would last.

The car sped through the night, its lights glowing on the dark stretch of road as the bright moon lighted the fields with a silvery brilliance. Time passed, stretching with the miles, and reason began to surface like a hungry wolf.

As they swung through the gates to his farm, they passed one of his men astride a horse, the dark silhouette of a rifle across his saddle. Cole tapped the horn lightly and the man waved.

The house still reeked of fried meat and french fries. The more time that elapsed, the more her doubts were increasing. Why had she consented? It was ridiculous, an open request for seduction. She paused in the dark kitchen.

Before she could say anything, Cole reached out and took her hand. His voice was husky in the quiet. "Don't say it, Marilee. I can feel the objection coming." Both arms slipped around her waist.

"You took advantage of me in the car," she said in a weak voice. "You knew you'd get what you want if you kissed me."

"All your resistance is on the surface, honey."

"And all yours is down deep where it counts."

"Shhh." He lowered his head, she raised her lips. She felt as if she had been waiting for his embrace ever since he last released her. Waiting for him, wanting him. She stepped closer to his strong, marvelous body as his arms tightened about her.

The magic flared between them just as it had on their first encounter. The spark that made her want him so achingly was still there. His hipbones were sharp against her, his hard thighs pressed hers with as much demand as his mouth.

He whispered in her ear, "I haven't rushed you. I've waited as long as humanly possible. . . ."

His thrusting, hungry kiss was more emphatic than his words. She trembled in his arms, feeling the joy of surrender. His kiss made her reel with pleasure, drove her to abandon. She wound her arms around his neck, arching to meet the body that felt so good against hers.

"You'll never know how I've had to fight to resist taking you." His voice held a rasp of yearning that shook her to her core.

His hands cupped her cheeks, tilting her face up. She closed her eyes, waiting, waiting . . .

She opened them, raising her lashes with an effort to find him watching her. "I want to see you look at me, to see in your eyes what I feel."

And she knew it was plain to him, bared to his view. No summer Kansas heat had the power to melt her as quickly as his gaze. Every pore, every inch of her quivered with the need for him, for the slow, languid strokes of his strong brown hands, the caresses that made her feel all woman, so necessary for his maleness.

With vivid clarity she remembered the first time, their evening beneath the stars. She was as lost now, made more vulnerable by memories.

Vaguely, she whispered, "For you I'll kiss my peace good-bye. I know you're another romantic disaster in my life."

"I'm not. This is so right. Tell me it isn't. Say it!"

Her lips raised, seeking his. She knew in her heart she couldn't mean more to him than a summer fling, a delightful interlude to be forgotten when he left Kansas. Whatever he felt, her heart was ensnared, bound deeper to him with every intimacy.

His hands moved over her cheekbones while his fingers wound in her hair. "You told me you were too old for dreams, but I'll show you that's not true."

He tugged the ribbon free and her hair swung over her shoulders. His hands slipped down her arms and around her waist to draw her to him again.

Her hands rested on his broad shoulders, itching to stroke his smooth skin. He tilted her chin up. "Kiss me, Marilee."

And she had to, wanted to eagerly. She raised her lips to meet his, to taste him. His mouth forcefully possessed hers. He held her close as one hand outlined her curves, drifting from her shoulder to her thigh, leaving a burning trail of need.

"I want you more than I've ever wanted anyone," he whispered hoarsely. "We'll be happy together."

She placed her finger on his lips. "Shh, Cole. Don't make impossible promises."

"Nothing is impossible. Your mildest kiss is a searing brand. You respond instantly. All afternoon, this evening, whenever I barely touch your fingers, your eyes darken . . ." He kissed her throat, his ragged voice as seductive as his work-roughened hands. "I couldn't stop touching you, couldn't resist watching your response, knowing you felt what I did. And you feel it now."

She couldn't deny his words. He was right.

"Since that first time, I haven't demanded more than you're willing to give." He buried his face in her soft hair, his lips teasing her neck, her shoulder. "I don't want to pressure you now." His tongue trailed over her collarbone, up behind her ear. "We'll take our time, but I want to love you until you're beyond reason. . . ." His lips sought the back of her neck. He lifted her hair away and nuzzled the sensitive skin there. "Until you're like you were that first night, a wild creature in my arms, a golden goddess."

His deep voice seemed to melt her very bones, turning them to a soft, pliable substance that weakly supported her. His voice, his lips, his hands swirled over her like a dense fog, barely touching, enveloping her in a mist of desire. Deeper than the agony for his touch came a soul searing emotional need for Cole. He banished her loneliness, the pain from old wounds. Relishing each brush of his mouth, she ached for him. She was drowning in sensation, a dual desire of her own and that primitive desire of all women to give the ultimate pleasure to the man they love.

Love! The thought dizzied her. She couldn't possibly love Cole. If she did, her future was hopeless.

But the future, the past fell away, lost to the moment, to the present need that heightened steadily. How much she wanted him! One night, a few hours. The same as that first evening. Could she lose herself to him again for a short time and still survive? While he held her as if she were a delicate flower, his hands resting on her hips, she tried to consider her question. There wasn't any debate over the answer. She wanted Cole. Totally.

Controlling himself with a supreme effort, he took his time, caressing her leisurely with mild, whispery kisses, gentle touches. He caught her hand, lifting her wrist to his mouth, reminding her of that first night when he had done just that at her front door. "Can you guess how much I've wanted you in my arms?"

Standing quietly in the dark kitchen, listening to his heartbeat, she wound her arms around his neck. "I've never known anyone like you, anyone who's affected me as you have. The more we're together, the more I need you."

A sharp yet sweet pain told her it would be so wonderful. He may not love her, but she would take the risk, would answer the unmistakable, age-less message in his blue eyes.

His fingers closed over the strap of her sundress, easing it down her shoulder while his gaze held hers and their breathing became labored. "How many times have you recalled that night, our lovemaking?" he asked.

"Too many," she whispered, scarcely aware of what she said. Suddenly the temperature in the kitchen was unbearable. It was a sultry heat that made her skin damp, yet she knew it was her own response making her body a furnace.

He slid the other strap over her bare shoulder. "Turn around," he commanded in a husky whisper.

She obeyed unthinkingly and his arm circled her waist. He kissed her shoulder as he pressed his body to hers, molding his front to her back. She could feel his strong legs, his male arousal. Cool air lazed over her moist skin as Cole swept her hair off the back of her neck, tasting her with his tongue and sending dazzling sparks down her spine.

She gasped with pleasure, closing her eyes, letting her head bow. His fingers brushed her back and his lips followed as he languidly tugged down the zipper of the sundress, baring her flesh to his seeking lips until he found her waist.

He released her hair and the thick auburn strands swung forward as he turned her to face him.

"Marilee, some things are hard for me to say. I've lived alone so much of my life. . . ."

It was difficult to follow his words, to forget his hands, to stop staring at his enticing mouth with firm lips that could be so very soft. . . .

He hit his chest lightly with his fist. "You fill something here, something I lack, some part of me. . . ."

If only she could believe him! He was speaking in a moment of passion, carried away no doubt by his hunger for her body. She could truthfully admit the same to him, but she was afraid to reveal how deep her feelings for him ran. She remained silent and his lashes drooped, half-covering his smoldering eyes.

He lazily pushed down the dark blue cotton dress, sliding it over her hips. She'd worn only filmy white panties beneath it. The dress fell unnoticed to the floor, then he hooked his fingers in the top of the panties and pulled them down until she stepped out of them.

She tilted her head back, gazing at him with narrowed eyes as his own blue eyes set her on fire.

His breathing was ragged, noisy in the silent kitchen. It was an effort to stand still, to wait and let him get his fill of looking at her. His languorous appraisal, drifting down, pausing, dropping lower, was as tangible as a caress. She longed to reach for him, to melt in his embrace.

"Cole . . ."

"Shhh. Wait, Marilee. I can't get enough of you. I want to look and then I want to touch, to kiss where my eyes and my hands have already explored, to kiss every inch of flesh until you can't be still, can't stand and wait and watch . . ."

She pushed off her sandals, then began unbuttoning his shirt, baring his tanned chest. Her gently exploring fingers discovered his wildly pounding pulse.

He swept her into his arms. His long strides carried them down the hall into the living room where he placed her on the wide rust velvet sofa. Then he straightened, standing tall beside her.

The material under her back was soft, the air cool on her skin, but nothing registered except her awareness of Cole's devouring gaze. He stepped back and sat on the edge of a dark brown chair. His gaze remained on her as he tugged off his black boots and socks.

She stood up when he did and pushed the shirt off his shoulders, her lips seeking the hollow of his throat, feeling the tiny sharp bristles of his beard as her lips traveled across his jaw to his mouth.

"Marilee . . ." He sighed her name, drawing out the word before his lips closed over hers in a heart stopping kiss that obliterated the world.

Fumbling with the heavy buckle, she unfastened his belt. His fingers shook as he unsnapped and unzipped his jeans, then he let them fall to the floor with a jangle of change.

He started to tug away his dark briefs, but Marilee's fingers accomplished the task, moving down his strong legs.

"Oh, Lord, how I need you!" He groaned. "I've wanted you desperately since that first night. You shattered my life when you dropped from the sky." He lay her down on the sofa and stretched out beside her.

He stroked her throat. "This is long enough to wait." His brown fingertips brushed the underswell of her thrusting breast, making her gasp with pleasure. "Too long! You don't know what effort it's taken, how much control I had to exert that first evening. . . ."

His kisses were brief, hard, tantalizing before he shifted and slipped off the sofa to kneel beside it, his eyes feasting freely on her, causing her to writhe beneath their provocative scrutiny.

He leaned forward to fondle her, to discover her intimately, to give her ecstasy. She moved off the sofa, coming down into his arms, feeling his bare legs beneath hers. For the first time in her life all inhibitions fell away. She wanted to explore his muscled body, to give him pleasure, to caress his hard lean frame that was so precious to her.

The moments stretched, lost in escalating seeking, touching intimacies that rocked them both, making their hearts pound as one. She knew when his control was slipping. His kisses became harsh demands, his body shook beneath her fingers.

They lay side by side on the floor, oblivious to its hardness or the scratchy beige carpet. Suddenly Cole cupped her face in his hands, leaning over her. "Now, love, do you believe in dreams?"

"Yes!" He had given her a dream of love, of fulfillment. She reached up to pull his head down. She didn't want distance between them, nothing. She wanted to envelop Cole, to be one with him. She had never felt such wild joyous abandon, such heartbreaking hunger for a man's body, his touch.

"Cole, please . . . I want all of you. I want to belong to you now."

He groaned hoarsely and shifted, stretching on his back and pulling her over him, crushing her to him, taking her in a hard male thrust that made her close her eyes with rapture. His hands stroked as their bodies fused, uniting.

She leaned down to kiss him, her dark red hair tumbling over their faces.

"Marilee, love . . ." he gasped. "I need you. Oh, love!"

She cried out as a wild sensation exploded within her. Cole's powerful frame shuddered. His hands closed about her waist, pulling her down.

She was lost, utterly lost in joy and hopelessness, pleasure and pain. . . .

Exhausted, she sprawled in complete abandon on his broad chest, listening to the wild drumming of their hearts as they slowed to normal. His skin was damp with perspiration, smooth and moist to touch. One strong arm was locked around her, pinning her to him. His other hand stroked the back of her head, smoothing her hair, lifting it off her neck, caressing her.

"That was good, love. So very, very good." He sighed and his hand moved lower to stroke her back as if she were a kitten.

She slipped to the floor beside him while he turned slightly. One arm still held her close, one long leg moving between hers, the other dropping over hers to hold her against his damp body.

He propped his head on his hand and brushed short hairs away from her face, then leaned down to touch her temples, her cheeks with his lips.

"Cole."

He paused, his face inches away.

"That was good. I . . . I haven't . . ." It was impossible to tell him she hadn't ever made love so rapturously with a man before. "It was special," she finished lamely.

He sat up to look at her and she lay still, enjoying his gaze wandering over her, feeling no embarrassment as she looked at him as eagerly. "Marilee—" He bit off the words. He rose abruptly and held out his hand. "Let's get that moonlight swim."

"I don't have the strength to stand," she whispered, taking his hand. He pulled her to her feet and scooped her into his arms.

"If you think *you* can't stand, this is a superhuman effort," he said, laughing softly.

"Put me down. I'll walk. I don't want you to collapse."

He moved through the darkened house and shouldered open the kitchen door, heading for the pool. He didn't slacken his pace when he reached it, but walked just as nonchalantly to the edge and dropped into the pool with Marilee still in his arms.

She screamed and tightened her hold around his neck, remembering just in time to close her mouth. The shock of cold water was delicious, perfect on her hot skin. She clung to Cole, tugging him down playfully until his strong fingers peeled her arms away and he shot to the surface.

She broke through the water and faced him laughing.

"Some thanks I get. I love you senseless and you try to drown me!" His grin belied his gruffness.

"That's why I did it. I don't have any sense left. You ruined me, my life, and I'm so bemused I don't know what I'm doing."

"You don't, huh." His hand moved playfully across her bottom. "Let's see . . ."

Splashing water on him, she swam out of reach.

He swam to the edge and tugged one of the rafts into the pool. "Come here, Marilee. I want you in my arms."

"We can't both get on that."

"Come here, woman, and stop arguing."

She swam over to him and he lifted her carefully up beside him. The raft bounced crazily, then settled as she lay back in the crook of Cole's arm, her head on his warm shoulder, one of her legs thrown over his. His arm held her close, his one hand resting on her bare midriff, his dark fingers splayed over her pale skin. The raft rose and dipped slightly as the waves in the pool settled. They gazed at an extravaganza of twinkling stars splashed overhead in the night sky. A brilliant white moon shone down, looking cold and remote above them.

"Cole, none of your men will come here, will they?"

"No, we have complete privacy. That's why I have high fences to keep everyone away."

She stared at the myriad of stars, watching them blink while his words echoed in her mind. "To keep everyone away." She sensed that, even in his most intimate moments, Cole still kept a barrier around himself, an invisible fence that kept anyone from becoming too much a part of his life, too important to him.

Regrettably, she didn't do the same.

"What's wrong?" he asked.

"Nothing."

"I heard a long sigh."

"I don't know. Perhaps it was satisfaction."

"Good."

"This is marvelous," she said, changing the subject. "It's unbelievably beautiful out here. How can you go back to Tulsa?"

She spoke without thinking. Only when there was a moment of silence did she realize that she may have intruded, may have sounded as if she wanted to hold him.

Reinforcing her conclusions, his muscles tensed slightly, but when he answered, his tone was casual. "My work is there. I can't farm and give up the other businesses. Someday I'd like to settle here, but not for years."

Why had she asked? Forget everything but now, she reminded herself. Everything but that his arms encircled her, his magnificent body lay against hers. They were happy and contented.

"See, you were wrong," she said.

"How's that?"

"About my hang-up over a nude male body."

He chuckled. "I cured you."

His arm tightened to hold her still as she started to wriggle in protest.

"Maybe you did," she conceded as her fingers started to caress him intimately.

"Don't start something you don't want to finish," he warned.

"Let's see. You said I was prudish, had hang-ups about nudity, was too modest. . . ." She twisted and raised slightly to look down at him. Moonlight bathed his features in a silvery glow and highlighted his taut muscles, powerful shoulders, flat smooth stomach. All the teasing left her as an ache started in her loins. She wanted to cherish his marvelous body, to explore it thoroughly again, to give him as much pleasure as possible. She leaned forward to trail her tongue over his chest. Instantly his arms closed around her and the raft started rocking.

"Be still," she whispered, twisting carefully to trace her lips over a bony hip. "Don't move or we'll be in the pool. Let me love you, Cole. Let me do this. I want to please you. . . ."

He groaned, hardening with desire, stroking her back to start the fires that would consume her.

In seconds they rolled into the water, tumbling down, their wet, slippery bodies moving together while Cole returned her caresses.

They bobbed to the surface to kiss, until finally Cole wrapped one arm around her and swam to the edge to get out and lift her up beside him. Together, leisurely, they moved to the chaise. He pulled her down beside him, stroking her cool wet skin until she was trembling with longing.

When she moaned softly, pulling him to her, he shifted her beneath him to possess her, this time taking her quickly, feverishly, his mouth plundering hers in hard kisses until she tore her lips from his to cry out in ecstasy.

Exhausted, they lay locked together. Cole's arm

tightened around her. "My darling witch," he murmured and closed his eyes.

She shifted to look at him, at the faint smile on his lips, the dark locks of hair plastered damply to his forehead, his broad chest rising and falling with deep, regular breathing. She settled against him, closing her eyes to let exhaustion take away her worries.

Later, she opened her eyes and stared blankly into the darkness, uncertain how much time had passed. She stirred and Cole's arm tightened around her. She gently pried his arm loose. She had to go home. Cole was like a drug to her system and she needed to get away to where she could view things rationally.

She crossed the darkened patio and entered the house. Upstairs she gathered her shorts and shirt from earlier in the day. As she leaned down in the darkened bedroom to pick up her sneakers, she glanced out the window and saw a light bobbing up and down at the corral.

Curious, she crossed to the window. A light switched on, catching the end of a cattle truck, then the light winked off and the truck was swallowed up in darkness.

Knitting her brow, she stared in the direction of the barns, the pen that held Bonny Charles. The pen with the bull. A chill ran down her spine. Suddenly, the shrill scream of an alarm shattered the stillness of the night.

Nine

While the siren's wail rose and fell, she continued
to stare outside for a stricken moment. Headlights blinked on, moving quickly away from the
pen that held Bonny Charles. She could clearly
see a small cattle truck when it passed beneath
the tall lamp post where the road circled away
from the barns and the corral. It had to be rustlers driving away with Bonny Charles!

If the truck was headed for the main road, it
would pass the house within minutes. Marilee
dashed downstairs to the back door to call, "Cole!
Cole!"

Above the sound of sirens, she couldn't hear
any answer.

"Cole!"

Panic filled her. Where were all the guards, his
massive protection? Where was Cole? She thought
of how soundly her father slept. Sirens, even an
explosion, might not wake him. She bit her lip.

She started for the pool, then heard a motor approaching in the distance and stopped. The truck would pass the house in seconds.

She whirled, dashing to the living room, and climbed onto a chair to snatch down the loaded pistol that Cole had shown her the first night. Surely, he'd wake in a minute. Maybe she could stop them until he or a guard came.

She glanced down at her naked body, then saw Cole's shirt lying on the floor. She snatched it up frantically. The truck was almost there.

Racing to the front door, she tried to remember what Cole had shown her about the gun.

The sirens should wake the dead. She made a mental note to fall in love next time with a light sleeper. Fall in love. Where was he? How could he sleep through such racket?

Holding the pistol, she couldn't pull the knit shirt over her head, so she wrapped it around her body, clutching it with one hand.

As the truck swung around a curve, the headlights struck the trunk of an elm at the front of the fenced yard.

She ran, breathless, sobbing in frustration, fear, and anger. Damn the man and his sleep! How did she release the safety? She tried to remember his strong, brown fingers handling the weapon, his brief instructions.

"Ouch!" she yelped, hopping on one foot for a moment when a briar pricked her skin. When she reached the gate, the truck was only yards away from the front of the house.

She said a small prayer that she could stop them and not kill someone or shoot off her toe. And then all rational thought was gone. She raced to the side of the road as the truck drew level, aimed at the tires, and pulled the trigger.

The sound deafened her and the recoil jerked

her hand. The truck sped along. With trembling finger she recocked the pistol, squeezed the trigger, closed her eyes, and fired.

She felt as if the moment were frozen in time. The bullet struck a tire! She had actually hit something!

The tire went flat, throwing the speeding truck out of control. It slewed around in three-quarters of a circle, sending a plume of dust into the air.

Marilee ran toward it until it came to a stop. Raising the heavy pistol, she leveled it at the truck, willing her arm not to shake or waver.

The doors opened and two men spilled out of the truck and rushed toward her.

Her hand ached and the pistol wavered wildly. She stepped into the full beam of the headlights and steadied the pistol with her last bit of fortitude.

"Halt, dammit," she shouted, "or I'll shoot!"

Both men stopped dead. Eyes bugging, their jaws hung open while they stared at her and the shirt wrapped haphazardly around her.

"Now look, lady," one of them began taking a step toward her.

The heavy pistol waggled in a zig-zagging arc. "Don't move! Get your hands up!"

Her veins turned to ice when she heard a rustle behind her, a low voice swearing steadily.

"Marilee, my God . . ."

"Where've you been!" she snapped without taking her eyes off the two men.

Cole snatched the pistol from her, steadying it on the men. "Hands higher!" he shouted, then said in a deadly quiet voice to Marilee, "Will you get your bare ass in the house! I'll do this!"

"Where the hell were you?" she asked, ignoring his command.

"Here comes Jack and Bill. Will you get inside?"

Raising her chin, she held on tightly to his

shirt and stepped out of the light. Merciful darkness enveloped her as she hurried inside. Her knees were shaking violently. Everything happened so fast, it was impossible to grasp the past few minutes. With one exception. "The next time I fall in love . . ."

She was in love with Cole Chandler! "Oh, dear God, here I go again," she groaned as she entered the dark living room.

Moving automatically, she flipped on lights, went upstairs, and dressed in her faded cut-offs, her shirt, and sneakers. Numbed, dazed, she worked with trembling hands. The past half-hour had left her dizzy with weakness, but she knew it wasn't because of the rustlers. It was Cole, her strong feelings for him. She leaned forward over a dresser and peered at herself in the oval mirror. Only one soft table light was on in the room. Outside, the sirens had stopped. The sound of men's voices, car engines, doors slamming, came clearly through the open windows. She barely noticed as she stared at the red hair tumbling over her shoulders, her wide green eyes, sunburned cheeks, and freckled nose.

"You've done it again, kid," she told the image. "Really done it this time. Before—that was puppy love. This is the real McCoy. Skyrockets," she said softly, brushing a tendril of hair away from her temple. "He's so appealing, so damned sexy. . . ."

"Now who could this conversation be about?" Cole drawled huskily behind her as his image joined hers in the mirror.

She watched his reflection as he walked across the room to stand behind her, his hands resting on her shoulders. He was bare chested and faded jeans covered his hips and long legs. Tousled locks of brown hair tangled enticingly over his forehead. Amusement, satisfaction, and something she couldn't fathom filled his blue eyes as he turned her to face him. "Marilee, you're something else. I've never known any other woman who would've confronted a bunch of rustlers."

His words mollified her embarrassment. Before she could answer, he added, "Are all your dates as exciting as ours have been?"

Attempting to forget the blush that consumed her, she asked, "Where were you?"

His expression changed, a definite twinkle appearing in his blue eyes. Here it comes, she thought, bracing for his teasing.

"Hon," he drawled, "the sheriff should hire you to catch all the criminals in the county. I mean those men were stupefied. They were zapped."

"Cole, so help me! I don't want to hear one word about it! If you hadn't been lollygagging, snoozing like the dead out by your pool—It's not funny!"

"I was dead because a red-haired witch had taken all my strength. Marilee, you're blushing!" He kissed her throat just above her collarbone.

"I've got to get home before Ted and Grant come by to pick me up for work."

"We'll hurry home in time for you to catch your ride back here," he murmured against her ear. Straightening, he smiled. "I have to go into town to make out a report about the attempted theft. I'll take you home on the way."

She bit her lip. "Will I have to testify or go or anything like that?"

He laughed. "I'll protect you from, er, exposure."

"Mr. Chandler, you're pushing your luck!"

Chuckling, he bit her ear lightly. "Don't worry. You won't be involved."

Her attention wandering badly, she let out a long breath of relief. She didn't want to encounter the rustlers again as long as she lived.

As if he read her mind, Cole said softly, "Honey,

don't worry, they'd recognize your luscious legs before they recognize your face."

"Dammit, Cole! Are you really that sound a sleeper?"

"Yep, 'fraid so. When I woke up, I took a few seconds to put on my pants." He grinned. "It just didn't occur to me to rush out there naked as a jaybird. I saw my pistol was gone, the front door was open, and I guessed where my pistol might be. Damn good shot."

"Thank you. I had my eyes closed."

Laughing, he gave her a swift hug that knocked the air out of her lungs. His breath stirred her hair as he said, "Seems I remember someone telling me about how ordinary and quiet a life she leads. . . ."

She pushed away from him. "It is, or was until you came along. And you never did answer my question that night."

She expected him to ask what question she meant, not to remember he hadn't answered when she had asked why he wasn't the marrying kind.

Instead his laughter vanished as he gazed down into her eyes. Abruptly, he said, "We better continue our conversation in the car or the sheriff will come looking for me."

He turned away, but not before she saw the darkening of his blue eyes, the cold shutter that dropped with finality over his expression.

While she watched him walk away from her, his smooth back rippling with muscles, his trim hips covered in low-slung jeans, his long feet bare, a pain started in her chest, in her heart, spreading its agony to the remotest parts of her being. She couldn't breathe, her face felt hot, her body ached, and she knew how far she had gone, how far she'd let him go with her. He'd seduced her, taken her body, her emotions, her heart, leaving an aching emptiness.

Without looking back Cole disappeared into the hall. She stayed rooted to the spot, staring into space, hurting and hurting.

The spell ended when she heard his call.

"Marilee!"

"Coming!" she answered, hurrying to the door. She looked back once, as if she had left something important behind and couldn't find it, then turned and went down the stairs to meet him.

The drive into Wichita was filled with silences between talk about the rustlers, about Bonny Charles, and the coming livestock show. Cole held her close against him. Even while she spoke with him, her mind kept replaying the last few minutes at his house. With her cheek against his hard shoulder, she gazed up at his profile, examining his features while she examined her feelings for him. She was in love with him, deeply, absolutely, too swiftly to comprehend. She wanted to bring it up again, to ask the questions that plagued her, but she didn't. He kissed her goodnight, dropped her off, and drove away.

During the remaining hours of the night she slept little and fitfully. Cole wasn't one for commitment. The rustlers—his sole reason for staying at the farm—had been caught. She had known him such a short time. Yet how devastating that time had been! She was in love with him. His image came to mind to torment her as she remembered all the little things about him that she loved: his sexy blue eyes, his laughter, his imagination, his gorgeous male body, his personality—every damn bit of him except his reluctance for any lasting ties. She tossed miserably in bed, finally rising to bathe and dress and go to work.

If Ted and Grant noticed her silence, they didn't

remark about it. Their talk drifted around her, some words registering, most lost. It was another hot June day, the temperature soaring into the nineties early in the morning.

When they stopped in the wide drive, she saw the empty garage and knew Cole was gone.

After working for several hours Ted and Grant followed the usual routine, swimming briefly before lunch. Marilee had lost her enthusiasm and just sat in the shade, sipping tepid cola and leaving her sandwich untouched.

They returned to scraping until the middle of the afternoon when the black Thunderbird roared into the garage.

Marilee's pulse jumped. Torn with a mixture of emotions, she scraped furiously.

"Hi."

There went her pulse, her breathing, her wits. He stood a few yards away beneath the shade of an elm. A stubble of whiskers darkened his jaw and his hair was a tangle of curls. His white shirt was rumpled, tucked into dark jeans.

"Where's Henry?" she asked, keeping her voice even with great effort.

"He's on the patio. Come down off the ladder. I want to show you something." As she laid the scraper on the ladder, she asked, "Are the rustlers in jail?"

"Yeah, at the moment."

Aware of his full attention, she climbed down and turned around to look at him curiously. Not until he reached for her did she guess what he intended. "You'll get chips of old paint . . ." she began in a weak attempt to ward him off.

He pulled her into his arms to kiss her and her heart went up in flames. The misery she had suffered the last hours dissipated immediately. While in his embrace, with his mouth demanding her total attention, everything became right again, perfect. She wrapped her arms around him and clung to him, aware in a dim corner of her mind that there might not be too many more times to hold him.

Finally he released her, gazing at her solemnly, a flake of white paint on his cheek. "I couldn't wait," he said huskily. "It's been eternity."

Her thudding heart pounded in her ears, her veins. It was impossible to talk. She studied his features as if trying to memorize them. Brushing away the speck, she said, "You have paint on your face."

He smiled, his fingers drifting over her cheek. "So do you. Henry's waiting."

"I'll put away my ladder."

"I'll do it. I'll see you after Henry's lesson."

It was an effort to walk away, to keep from reaching for him. He had come into her life like a whirlwind, taken her heart, and now was about to rip it away. The same pain she had felt since the night before returned.

When she entered the patio and Henry wasn't in sight, she went inside to wash and clean up.

Returning to the patio, she found it still empty. "Henry!"

"Yes, ma'am."

Startled, she looked up to see Henry sitting on a high branch of a sycamore overlooking the patio. He started down the tree so she sat down and pulled her materials out of her bag. It was hot even in the shade, and since this was Jada's day off, there were no glasses of cool lemonade. Marilee pushed wisps of hair away from her forehead and looked around when Henry banged the gate.

Grime covered his face and blue t-shirt. The shoestrings of his frayed sneakers trailed along with each step until he climbed into a chair across from her.

He seemed as unenthusiastic as she when Marilee handed him a book, asking him to read.

Henry wriggled, placing a dirty forefinger beneath the line as he read.

Each word was faltering, some wrong. She frowned, watching him. He was reading far worse than before. "Henry, don't you want to read today?"

His blue eyes stared solemnly at her. With a shock she realized he had been crying. His cheeks were smudged, his eyes red. When he'd entered the patio, she'd been too busy getting out the books to notice.

He didn't answer, so she repeated her question. This time he shook his head, looking as miserable as she felt.

Marilee forgot her own troubles. "Henry, come here." Scooting over to make room, she patted the seat beside her. Henry squeezed in next to her. Marilee pulled out a new comic book, placing her arm around him.

"Want me to read to you today?"

He nodded, so she opened the comic and started on a tale about dragons. She hadn't finished the first page when she heard a sniff.

She looked down to see him brush at his cheek with his fist. She patted his shoulder. "Henry . . ." A shudder rippled the thin shoulders. "Henry, what's wrong? What's the matter?"

He hunched over, balling his fists against his eyes. "I want a daddy. Mom wants to get married and Uncle Cole won't let her!"

Stunned, Marilee smoothed his curls with a gentle hand. "He can't stop your mother from getting married."

"Yes, he can. He doesn't like Don. He told Mom she . . ." His voice broke on a sob and Marilee waited for him to get control of himself again. Her heart felt as if someone were grinding it into the dust. With a deep breath, Henry continued, ". . . was a fool to get married. He said it would only bring her trouble. They had a big fight."

"Henry, oh, Henry." Marilee hugged him as she stared blankly across the patio. She wanted to sob too. She fished a handkerchief out of her purse and pushed it in his hand. "Here."

He brushed away the handkerchief so she dropped it into her lap. His small frame shook while he cried. "Uncle Cole said marriage is trouble and misery. He's gonna talk her out of it and I still won't have a daddy."

"You have your Uncle Cole."

"He'll go. He always goes. He won't take us with him."

"If your mother really loves Don, she'll make up her own mind."

"Uncle Cole said she shouldn't have married the other times and she yelled at him that she wouldn't have me if she hadn't. . . ."

Damn Cole anyway. "Henry, where were you when they argued?"

"In the hall some of the time. Uncle Cole came for breakfast this morning. They didn't know I was awake."

"Henry, your uncle loves you very much."

He sniffed. After a moment he mumbled, "He doesn't like Don."

"Do you?"

"Yep."

"Does your mother?"

"Yep. She loves him. Uncle Cole said she always thinks she's in love. He said it won't last, marriage is a trap. It'll hurt her and me. It won't! I know it won't. He says it hasn't brought anyone in our family any good."

Oh, Lord. Marilee felt crushed. "Henry, your uncle loves you very much. He wouldn't have hired me to tutor you if he wasn't very interested in your welfare." She squeezed his shoulder. She wanted to pull him into her arms and hold him, but she suspected it would embarrass him.

Henry sniffed, rubbing his sneakers together while he stared at the ground. "He'll make Mom get rid of Don and then he'll go and we'll be alone again. He's gonna leave."

Something happened to her breathing as she felt a cold stab in her heart. "When's he going?" She hated asking Henry, but she couldn't resist.

"Day after tomorrow."

A wave of agony swept through her. Unaware of how long she'd sat in stunned silence, she came out of her reverie when Henry coughed. She looked down at his hunched shoulders.

"Henry, would you rather ride Blaze today than have a reading lesson?"

He glanced up and her heart felt as if it were breaking. His blue eyes were wide, filled with hurt. A tear spilled over onto his mud-streaked face, where tears had already run across the grime. He wiped it away hastily. Suddenly she could picture Cole as a child, see him hurt as badly as Henry.

She ached for him, for Henry, for herself.

Henry said, "I can't ride Blaze unless Uncle Cole is along."

"I'll get your Uncle Cole. Come on, let's wash your face and get a drink of cold water."

As soon as she had bathed away some of the grime and given Henry a glass of iced water, she sent him to the patio to wait.

With leaden steps, she walked to the foot of the stairs and called, "Cole!"

A husky voice drawled, "Hi."

She twisted to look above her. Cole was leaning

over the rail, gazing down at her, his broad shoulders, sexy blue eyes, his strong hands and lean body all conveying a vigorous, appealing masculinity that brought a tightness to her heart. She tried to ignore her automatic physical reaction to him. When her gaze met his, the smile on his face vanished. "Hey, what's wrong?"

"May I talk to you a minute?"

He came down the stairs and her despair deepened. Her heart skipped a beat at the sight of him. He had bathed and was dressed in snug jeans, boots, and an unbuttoned plaid shirt with the shirttails hanging out. His unruly hair was blown dry and combed into waves, except for a few curling, wet tendrils above his collar. She loved him. Totally. It was that simple and that terrible.

Buttoning his shirt, he descended and stopped in front of her. The top three buttons were still unfastened, revealing his broad chest with its dark hairs. She longed to reach for him, to touch him, to put her arms around him. Instead, she asked quietly, "Can we go somewhere private to talk?"

He motioned toward the living room, closing the door behind them. He put his hands on her shoulders as he gazed solemnly at her. "What's happened?"

Ten

"Henry overheard your argument with his mother this morning."

"Oh, Lord." He grimaced. "I thought he was asleep." His blue eyes searched hers.

"I told him you'd take him to ride Blaze."

"I think something else is bothering you."

"He's been crying."

Cole flinched and she wished she hadn't had to tell him. "I wouldn't hurt Henry for the world," he said gruffly.

"He said he likes Don. He wants a father."

"Sandy is gullible, she's vulnerable."

And so am I! she wanted to shout. "Don't you think Sandy ought to decide whether she'll marry or not?"

"Look, I'm the one who always has to pick up the pieces. Why do you think all her dresses are at the farm? Where do you think she goes when her world collapses?"

The hard look in the blue eyes she loved drove her beyond control. "It's too damn bad she's isn't invincible, completely self-sufficient like her brother!"

His blue eyes became glacial. "Marilee, I warned you that first night," he said quietly. "What we have together is marvelous. I want you now, but there's a part of me that just can't give. It isn't in me. I've been alone too many years, for so damn long, I can't remember when I depended on someone else for an emotional need. What family I have, depends on me. I had to be that way to survive, to take care of Sandy when we were kids, and now to take care of Henry. Whether I like it or not, my self-sufficiency has lasted."

"You're leaving this week."

"I'll be back now and then. Oh, honey, I don't want to hurt you. . . ."

But you don't need me, she thought. "Cole, Henry needs you badly. Will you see about him?"

"I will in a moment. Marilee, it's been so good. What we feel is special. . . ."

His voice dropped to the husky note that could always send a shiver down her spine. She wanted Cole. In spite of everything, knowing that he'd never need her as she did him, she wanted him. "Please, see about Henry."

For an instant she faced the unfathomable blue of his eyes, like an opaque sea. Then Cole turned.

"We'll talk later, Marilee."

He left, the door standing open behind him. She waited without moving until she was certain both he and Henry would be gone. As she started outside, Grant entered the patio.

"Time to go. Are you ready?"

"Yes."

"Anything wrong, Marilee?"

She shook her head. "No. Nothing at all." Nothing except the broken heart that had been inevitable since Cole's first kiss.

She climbed into the truck and sat between Grant and Ted. As they followed the flat road to the gate they saw two riders leaving the barn. Cole swept off a broad-brimmed hat to wave at them. Grant tapped the horn. Inside of Marilee, a small voice said good-bye to Cole. She knew she would see him again, but their brief affair was over.

As soon as she reached home, she peeled off her clothes and bathed in a cool tub. Afterwards, dressed in cut-offs and the yellow halter she'd worn the day she'd fallen into Cole's pool, she fixed a tall glass of iced tea and caught her hair up to fasten it on top of her head. She sat down in front of the papers piled on the kitchen table. Cole had cost her time when she should have been home working on her manuscript. He had cost her more than time. She stared at the wall and realized the cruise didn't hold any charm for her. Nothing but sexy blue eyes, Cole's strong arms, his companionship had fascination for her now.

She blinked back tears. Damned if she would cry over him like Henry had! Not at all. She wiped a tear off the paper under her hand and tried to concentrate. Oh, yes, Cole Chandler had cost her dearly. She shouldn't let him delay the textbook, mess up her career too!

It was an effort to concentrate for more than a few minutes at a time. She couldn't stop thinking about Henry, about Cole. Cole would leave soon, be out of her life forever unless she wanted bits and pieces of him if he came to stay at the farm again. No thanks. Could she resist even bits and pieces? She wiped her damp brow and checked the thermostat, moving it again.

By nine o'clock that night she knew with certainty that her air conditioner wasn't working. Hot and miserable, she rummaged through the garage for a fan and set it beside the desk while she tried to type.

One hour, four finished pages, and eighteen discarded ones later, the doorbell rang.

Marilee opened the door to face Cole. Dressed in the same plaid shirt and jeans he'd had on earlier, he looked cool, handsome, and immaculate. A black Stetson was pushed to the back of his head over a tangle of curls. His gaze swept over her and his eyes narrowed. "Are you all right?"

"I'm fine." That was a whopper. "What do you want?"

His eyes narrowed a fraction more. "May I come in?"

"Sure." She stepped aside to let him enter.

"Damnation. Do you have the furnace on?"

She wiped her forehead and neck. For a moment she had forgotten the heat. "My air conditioner broke."

"For heaven's sake. Why didn't you tell me?"

"It just happened an hour ago. Why should I tell you?"

"Come out to the farm until you get it fixed. With the weather we've been having, there's probably a waiting list for repairs."

"Thanks, but I need all my notes."

As she talked his gaze traveled past her, taking in her surroundings, and she realized he hadn't been in her house before.

"We'll take your notes."

"That's impossible." The good-bye had to come. She steeled herself to face him, to get through the next few minutes.

"Show me your notes."

"I'll stay here and practice some of your damned self-sufficiency."

His gaze returned to her, settling with a jarring intensity as his eyes narrowed. She wished she hadn't said it and added quickly, "I won't get any work done if I'm at your house."

"I won't disturb you. I'll be in Tulsa. I have to be there in the morning, sooner than I expected."

Her temper snapped. "I don't want to come to your house, to look at your things and long for you, your touch, your smile, your company!"

"Oh, honey, I'm sorry. Let's go where it's cool, where we can talk rationally."

"Is this how you always tell your women good-bye? Leave the broken hearts strewn behind like old flowers?"

She knew the accusation was unfair, but everything hurt. She was hot and miserable and suffering. Her temper, her patience had burned away. Cole had started toward her, but at her angry words he halted, a flush darkening his cheeks. For a long moment they stared at each other.

When he spoke, his voice was harsh. "I didn't mean to hurt you. We've had something good between us. I just can't help what I am, Marilee. If I asked you to go to Tulsa with me, you wouldn't be happy. Would you give up your work and go?"

"No," she answered swiftly. "Because in a few weeks you'll go to Alaska and I'll return to teaching. It would be good-bye then, so it'll be easier now." She held her breath for an agonizing second, waiting, hoping he might refute her statement, say they wouldn't part at the end of the summer. He didn't and her tiny hope crashed to pieces.

Instead he said, "Come to Tulsa until summer is over. I want you."

" 'Until summer is over . . .' No thanks. So there's

nothing more to say. I couldn't bear to stay at your house. I'd rather move into a motel."

He drew a sharp breath. "If that's what you want . . ." He turned and left. Cole vanished out of her life as swiftly as he had entered it. Their good-bye had been quick and simple. The hurt was monumental.

She let the tears fall unheeded, staring at the door. Suddenly, she started to rush after him, to see if she could catch him. A few more weeks with him in Tulsa was better than nothing.

With her hand on the doorknob, she halted. It would be worse and hurt more to say good-bye later after weeks with him. Leaning her forehead against the door, she listened to the Thunderbird start and drive away.

Finally she walked back into the kitchen and stared at her papers while long minutes ticked past. She wanted to dump all her work into the trash. It held no interest at all. Only one thing in the world was important, and he was gone.

She picked up the phone to dial her parents and ask if she could spend the night where there was air conditioning. Then she reconsidered, riffled through the phone book, called a Holiday Inn, making reservations for a room.

She fed the dogs, packed, and moved to the motel. Half a dozen times that night she reached for the phone, wanting Cole so badly that she was willing to take whatever she could get. But each time she stopped, dredging up all the logical reasons to resist calling him. There would be a good-bye between them eventually. He had made that all too clear. Now would cause less pain. But how could the hurt be any greater? Marilee slept finally, still dressed, sitting in a chair. She woke early and returned home.

The next days blurred, running together. Cole

had already left for Oklahoma when she, Grant, and Ted showed up for work that next morning. They finished scraping and finally painted his house. By working feverishly every spare moment she had finished her text before the deadline, but the effort drained her. All her enthusiasm was gone.

Gone just as surely was her interest in the cruise. She wanted to cancel, but it would place a financial hardship on Gina and Karen since she'd shared expenses with them. Besides, while nothing could alleviate her suffering, she might as well sit on a beautiful tropical beach as stay in blistering, dry Kansas.

She had continued tutoring Henry, who showed the marked improvement she had predicted to Cole, for as soon as Cole left town she discovered that Henry and Sandy lived in Wichita. They changed their schedule and she tutored Henry in her own home up until three days before the cruise. From Henry she learned that Sandy had an engagement ring and planned to get married the first week in September, and that one of Cole's men had taken Bonny Charles to Kansas City to the livestock show where he'd won first place.

A few days before she was due to fly to Miami she received an envelope post marked Tulsa, Oklahoma. She studied the scrawled handwriting for several minutes before opening the envelope. She pulled out a folded piece of paper and two checks fluttered to the floor.

Cole's message was brief. "Hi, hon. Miss you. Love, Cole."

Torn with agony, with longing for him, she gazed at the note for a long time. Finally she picked up the two sizable checks, one to be split among herself, Grant, and Ted, and the other for her tutoring. The latter was more than they had agreed upon.

She hugged his note to her heart, wanting any part of him. Then she carefully set it where she could glance at it while she packed for the cruise.

The time to leave finally arrived. Dressed in beige slacks and a matching blouse, Marilee settled in to her window seat beside her two friends, Karen and Gina. As they took off and the plane rose above Wichita, heading east, she glanced down.

Harvested fields of yellow stubble spread below. They flew over a sprawling house with a bright blue swimming pool and she was enveloped in agony, remembering Cole's deep blue eyes, his hard, tanned body, his teasing companionship.

For the thousandth time she reminded herself that she had known from the start that it wouldn't last. She felt a jab in her side and turned to face her blond companion.

Karen Franklin stared intently at her. "Marilee, what's the matter with you? You only hear half our conversations."

"I'm sorry."

"You act like you haven't climbed out of bed. Do you have your itinerary? Mine's in my suitcase."

"It's right here." She rummaged through her purse and handed the itinerary to Karen.

Gina leaned closer to Karen to read with her.

"Imagine being in Miami in such a short time," Gina said. "I hope I get such a tan that it won't fade until next April!"

Marilee smiled at the dark-haired woman. Gina was as dark as Karen was blond.

"I can't wait to meet some gorgeous hunk on shipboard," Gina continued. "I hope he's six feet four, has golden hair, and blue eyes."

"Good!" Karen said. "That leaves the tall, dark,

silent type for me." She glanced at Marilee. "What's your type, Marilee?"

"I'm sorry, what did you say?"

"Where are you? What type of man appeals to you? We better know before we get on that cruise ship. We'll know what or who to look for."

"I'll leave all the men on shipboard to the two of you."

"Then why're you going on a cruise?" Gina asked. "I'm looking for the future Mr. Whatever-His-Name-Is."

Smoothing a wayward tendril back into the bun on top of her head, Marilee smiled. "I'm going to rest, swim, look at green trees and green grass and blue water. Anything besides wheat and dry ground."

"I find that a little hard to believe," Gina said, eyeing Marilee curiously.

"You know Marilee means what she says."

"No woman in her right mind means that! You'll change when we get on board."

They landed in Miami and checked into their hotel. Marilee declined an evening of sightseeing, telling her friends truthfully that she had a headache. The next day they left for their ship.

Dressed in a green and white striped cotton dress with a thin green belt and white pumps, Marilee rode quietly in their taxi to the dock. At the sight of the Aphrodite Oceanis, the beautiful white ocean liner riding at anchor, her spirits remained at a low ebb. She climbed the gangplank, listening to her friends' conversation, while part of her remained lost in memories of various moments spent with Cole, of his deep-throated laugh, his passionate lovemaking. She had been hurting so steadily and relentlessly, she wondered if she would ever get over the wound. As she trailed quietly behind Gina and Karen, she compared herself to her two companions.

Both of them were younger. Gina had just finished her second year as a Latin teacher and Karen had finished her fourth year as a home economics teacher.

While they were all good friends at school, Marilee found it impossible to share in Karen and Gina's enthusiasm now. The prospect of meeting entertaining men on the cruise was obviously uppermost in their minds. And she knew they didn't believe her when she said she wasn't interested.

As they boarded the ship, Karen grabbed Marilee's arm. "There! look, the perfect man! Let's all say a short prayer he's single."

Marilee smiled, feeling ancient. "You two are hopeless! You can stand here and drool over every handsome male all you want, but I'm going to look at the stateroom."

She located their cabin and started to unpack, but instead sat down on the bunk and stared into space, her mind far away. What was Cole doing? Was there another woman in his life now?

That hurt too badly to contemplate. She lost track of time until a knock stirred her. Karen and Gina burst in, each taking one of her arms.

"We're going to sail," Gina said. "You have to come watch."

"And guess what?" Karen asked brightly. "Without waiting for Marilee to guess, answered her own question. "The entire Fort Lauderdale water polo team is on board. Isn't that marvelous?"

"I'm so glad, Karen," Marilee said absently. She wondered if Cole was still in Oklahoma. Her thoughts drifted from the conversation around her.

"Wait 'til you see a blond giant named Willie."

"I'd rather stay here." She tried to pay attention to Gina.

"You've been teaching too long. It did something to your brain this winter."

"Are you well, Marilee?"

"I'm fine. I'm just not interested in man-hunting, ladies."

"You're not interested in anything!" Karen exclaimed. "What's happened to you? You don't eat, you don't sleep, you can't keep your mind on anything!"

Marilee shrugged. "Sorry. I don't want to put a damper on your fun."

"You won't," Gina said. "But you have to watch us sail. Come on."

Reluctantly, she went with them. Standing at the rail on deck, she gazed at Miami, then up at a blue, blue sky. But it only reminded her of Cole's blue eyes. "Marilee, here they come!" Gina hissed, then said, "Hi. Here's our friend."

Gina introduced Marilee to one tanned, fit handsome member of the water polo team after another, yet they might as well have been posts for all the interest they stirred in Marilee. The men crowded to the rail around the three women and talked to Gina and Karen. Marilee only noticed the vibrations that the ship's engines sent through the deck as they sailed slowly away from the dock. The wind caught wispy tendrils of her hair, blowing them against her cheeks. Ignoring the farewell shouts, the conversations swirling around her, the sunshine beating down, Marilee clung to the rail and stared into the murky water below.

Cole. Could she ever forget him?

Nothing held importance any longer. Not one single thing.

Miami dwindled to almost nothing as the gap of water widened. A large ship passed them, heading into the dock, its whistle drowning out all conversation momentarily.

Suddenly Gina pointed toward the shore and said, "Hey, look! They're headed for our ship."

Marilee turned to see a small launch approaching, cutting through the blue water and sending a spray of white behind it as it sped toward them.

"Someone who missed the boat," one of the polo team said and everyone laughed.

The launch raced toward them, its bright flags fluttering. Two men stood in the bow and another sat at the stern. High above its brown deck a gull circled, spreading its wings and rising on air currents.

In a few seconds the launch cut its motor and slowed its approach, swinging in a wide circle to come alongside the ocean liner. Marilee glanced idly beyond them to the faintly visible Miami skyline.

Over a megaphone came a loud, clear call. It rang across the narrow expanse of water between the launch and the ship, carrying clearly over the babble of conversation at the rails.

"Marilee O'Neil! Marilee O'Neil!"

Eleven

Shock. Shock froze her, numbed her. She stiffened, her gaze moving to the launch, to the two men standing in the bow.

And then the sun came up in her world. She wanted to shout, to jump up and down, to climb over the rail and fling herself into the ocean in front of the small craft. Cole. His dark hair was blowing in the wind. He was half-turned from her, standing with that familiar, unforgettable air of authority with one hand on his hip. Dark glasses hid his eyes. His white shirt sleeves whipped against his long arms and the ends of a navy tie fluttered slightly. Cole. Everything inside her came to life.

"Marilee, that's you they're calling!" Gina said.

"Cole!" Marilee yelled. Everyone around her turned to stare as she waved frantically, but her cry and gesture were lost in the mass of people.

The man with a megaphone standing beside Cole, called her name again.

"What've you done, Marilee?" Karen asked. "Who is that?"

Marilee wanted to sing, to laugh with glee. "Cole!" She turned and grabbed the arm of the man beside her. "You guys, will you please call to him. His name is Cole Chandler."

The tall blond next to her grinned. "Sure thing."

In unison, the entire Fort Lauderdale water polo team shouted, "Cole Chandler!"

His dark head turned and Marilee waved wildly. Her heart thudded against her ribs as his hand raised and he waved in return.

"Marilee! Who is that?"

"I'll tell you later." She watched as the launch came alongside and Cole started up the rope ladder.

They met amidship in a throng of people, but no one else existed for Marilee. One look at Cole's irresistible smile, his long, hard body, and she forgot the world. Cole reached for her and she went into his arms, into his heart forever.

Holding her tightly, he tilted her chin up and kissed her. When he released her, she reached up to remove his sunglasses, then stared into his marvelous blue eyes in stunned silence.

"Come on," he said, his voice gruff. "I've only a few minutes to get you off this ship. Get your things while I find the captain."

She didn't question him or hesitate. Nothing mattered except Cole. She didn't care if he wanted to see her for just a few days. She had to go with him.

She rushed to the cabin with Gina and Karen trailing behind. "Marilee, what are you doing?" Karen asked.

"Aren't you going on the cruise?" Gina said.

"Who's Cole Chandler?"

"He's gorgeous! Marilee, I think you've held out on us."

"I'm sorry," Marilee said hurriedly over her shoulder. "I'll write and explain. I can't now. Cole said to meet him." She snatched up her purse and bag and rushed back to find him waiting with the captain.

Marilee said good-bye to Karen and Gina, listened to Cole talk to the captain, and climbed into the launch without a glimmer of what she was doing.

As they stepped down into the rocking launch, the crowd on deck shouted, "Good-bye, Marilee! Good-bye, Cole!"

Cole grinned and waved with her while the launch started and turned to speed back to Miami. They couldn't talk above the roar of the launch's motor, but Cole held her close until they reached the dock.

Within minutes they stepped ashore on the dock at Miami. Cole tipped the men who had brought them ashore, shook hands, and thanked them. The sun was bright and warm. People were milling about them and somewhere nearby a ship's whistle blew.

As the two men left them, Cole set her suitcase down on the dock and turned to her.

"Will you marry me?" he asked.

Out of the corner of her eye, Marilee saw a few heads turn their way. She didn't care.

"What happened to your damned self-sufficiency?" she said. More heads turned and Cole's white teeth flashed.

"It left with a gorgeous redhead."

She folded her arms across her chest. "And that song and dance you gave Sandy about marriage being 'trouble and misery'?"

Cole's expression grew somber. "Please understand, Marilee. My parents' marriage was awful and I've seen Sandy go through two heart wrenching divorces. Is it any wonder I was a little skeptical about marriage?"

"And now?"

He took a deep breath. "And now I've found a woman I can't live without, a woman I want beside me all the time, a woman I need, I—"

"Oh, Cole!" She had waited as long as possible. As she rushed into his arms, she cried, "Yes! Oh, yes, I'll marry you."

He leaned down to kiss her and she knew she could never get enough of him, not even in a lifetime. When he finally released her, he glanced around. "Let's get out of here. We can talk where it's private."

He hailed a taxi and as they sped toward the airport, he pulled her to him.

"Will you tell me what we're doing?" she asked as she nestled against him.

"He grinned, making her heart pound faster and her whole body long to be wrapped around him.

"Honey, when I blew a fifty thousand dollar deal because I couldn't keep my mind on simple little details, I knew I needed you desperately."

She met his blue eyes, then glanced at the cab driver. "Cole, I wish you wouldn't say things like that to me in public."

He pulled her closer. "Who cares? I love you. I need you. Marilee, I couldn't sleep. I couldn't work. I couldn't eat. . . ."

Every sentence filled her with joy. She ran her finger down his cheek, noticing for the first time that he did look thinner. "I know," she whispered. "Why didn't you just call and ask me to skip the cruise?"

"I told you, I'm old enough to be set in my ways.

It didn't get through my thick skull what I was suffering from until after you'd gone. I've been to Kansas. I've chased all over the country for you."

His blue eyes enveloped her in their depths. She forced her attention back to the matter at hand. "Would you mind telling me our schedule? My family might like to know."

"Oh, here." He started to reach into his pocket, then stopped. "Never mind. We'll be catching a plane for Kansas so you can see your family, get your things, and get married. I have to be in Alaska a week from today. Think you'll like Alaska for a few weeks?"

"I think I will. Cole, what's in your pocket?"

He grinned. "We'll wait for a romantic setting."

"I don't think I want to wait. You're here, that's enough."

His blue eyes darkened and he reached into his pocket. "This isn't what I planned"—his blue eyes twinkled—"but then with you, nothing ever is!"

"Oh, really?" She watched as he withdrew a small box and placed it in her hand.

"I love you, Marilee."

He was solemn, his eyes filled with an unmistakable need. His voice deepened with a vulnerable note she hadn't heard before. "I need you, desperately. You gave me something, Marilee, that I haven't found before. I can let down completely with you, trust you with everything. I've missed you, your laughter, your kisses. . . . What we found was so special. I only feel that way with you."

She felt as if she would burst with joy. Never had she dreamed Cole would return her own feelings so strongly.

He caressed her cheek with his warm hand. "That day you crashed into my pool, you came down past all the barriers. The ones on my farm and the ones in my heart. I've had to be independent for so long, Marilee, so damned long. When you left, I finally realized that I needed you, your laughter, your love—"

"Oh, Cole! You're not the only one. I haven't been the same either." He crushed her to him for another hungry kiss until she shifted to ask, "You'll never know what a shock it was to hear my name called like that!"

He chuckled. "I couldn't just saunter up and tap you on the shoulder. I wanted your full attention."

"You have it, now and always."

"Sure enough, luv." He grinned at her and Marilee grinned back. She felt like laughing deliriously, like crying for joy. She trailed her fingers down his throat.

"We won't be alone until when?"

"Too damn long. Hours from now. We'll just have to make the best of a hardship." He pulled her to him and kissed her fiercely. When he released her she opened the box and gazed tearfully at the glittering diamond inside.

Twelve

"Cole, look!" Marilee stepped out of the truck and flung herself into a snowbank, relishing the cold. She stood and shook the snow off her skirt, feeling it fall over her stockinged legs and pumps.

Cole climbed down from the truck, the wind whipping the fur parka around his face while he carried their suitcases to the door of the small cottage.

"They promised to have this ready for us," he said. "They better have kept their word or heads'll roll." He disappeared inside.

Oblivious of her cold legs and high heels, Marilee stomped through the snow, pausing with her hands on her hips to survey the Alaskan scene. They were above the timberline; on the mountainsides below were tall dark green pines The rustic log cottage had a wide roof that sloped down to hang over the porch. Behind the house was a small barn and corral, a garage for the truck, and a toolshed. She raised her head to look at the snowy mountains, the brilliant blue sky overhead. The wind swept up the snow, swirling flakes into the air.

Her shadow was dark over the sparkling snow. She kicked her foot, sending a spray of snow flying. Movement caught her eye and she looked up to see a plume of gray smoke curl out of the chimney.

She walked in a circle, making tracks, waiting for Cole to return.

"Marilee."

He stood on the porch, his blue eyes squinting in the bright light. He looked so masculine, his hands on his hips as if he owned all he surveyed, he made her heart lurch violently.

"Hey, handsome!" she called. "I've got everything now. Snow, a sexy male . . ."

He took the two porch steps in one leap, strode rapidly along the walk to her, scooped her into his arms, and headed for the house again.

"I thought you'd never come out of there," she teased.

"I had to get a fire roaring to take the chill off and set the mood."

"I don't think you'll have to be too concerned with chills or mood."

"Is that so?"

"Yep. You see, I have this craving for your gorgeous body." His deep blue eyes were so filled with love that she caught her breath. "Oh, Lord, how I love you!" she said huskily, tugging his face down to kiss him.

They kissed for long moments, oblivious to the cold, of anything until Marilee became aware of the layers of clothing that were a barrier. As if he felt the same, Cole raised his head, his smoldering gaze sending her pulse into flight.

His voice was gruff, husky, and sensual. "Honey, I have the same damn craving for you. I can't wait to see your green eyes darken, to know you need me. . . ."

She buried her head against his throat and clung to him while he carried her over the threshold into the living area. Braided rugs covered the polished floor and a fire was roaring in the stone hearth.

Cole kicked the door closed behind him and set her on her feet. He slipped his hands over the collar of her coat, peeling the coat away and letting it drop to the floor. "Welcome home, Mrs. Chandler."

Her heart thudding wildly, she wound her arms around his neck. "Welcome home yourself, Mr. Chandler."

"Want to see your new home?"

With each word his voice deepened. She looked into his deep blue eyes, then her gaze dropped to his firm jaw sprinkled with dark bristles.

"I need to shave."

"Hmmm? Not necessarily."

"We've flown all night. Do you know how long it's been since I had you to myself? Completely to myself?"

He pulled a pin from the bun on top of her head, then another, and a long lock of auburn hair tumbled over her shoulder.

"You have me now." It was an effort to keep her eyes open, to talk. She tilted her face upward, wanting his mouth on hers.

"There. Your eyes are a deep green." As he pulled the remaining pins from her hair, letting auburn curls cascade over her shoulders, she studied each feature of his face, his prominent cheekbones, the thick fringe of curly lashes. His beloved face, hers now and forever.

"Are you going to show me around?"

"Sure." His lashes lowered over smoldering blue eyes.

He stripped off the white jacket of her suit. Over twelve hours ago in the church dressing room in Wichita, she had changed from her white satin wedding dress to the suit.

He kissed her throat, her lips, brushing her mouth with his as he tugged at the ends of the pale blue silk bow of her blouse. His parka fell beside hers and he shrugged out of his light suit coat and tossed it onto a chair.

With each passing second her heartbeat accelerated. How handsome Cole looked! She was aching with longing for him.

The single button at her waist went, the zipper next, then the skirt was a whisper over her hips.

"Everything's here, luv," Cole whispered. "A place for you to type and work on your next textbook, a kitchen, a bathroom, and a bedroom."

Her fingers twisted his narrow gold belt buckle, slipping it free. She slid her hands over his hard chest to unfasten his tiny shirt buttons while he removed his gold cuff links. The gold band on his finger glittered with his movements.

"I'll show them to you," he continued, "but not in that order."

"I can't wait. It's wonderful . . ." She pushed his shirt off his shoulders as he leaned down to kiss her throat, to trail enticing kisses to her ear, to tease the corner of her mouth with his tongue. "Lord, how I need you," he murmured. "I couldn't face coming up here without you. I couldn't bear another day without you. You don't know how many nights I stayed awake wanting you. Marilee . . . my life changed that day by the pool, changed forever, for the better."

"It's mutual, Cole." She closed her eyes, tilting

her head back, making her hair swing free behind her head.

Cole's hand slipped around her waist as he pulled her to him to kiss her. Her mouth opened eagerly as she returned his kisses.

After a few minutes he lifted his head. "I wish I hadn't had to rush you."

"Do you now?"

A brief smile flicked across his features. His chest heaved as his eyes devoured her. His voice was raspy. "No more hang-ups?"

She smiled, looking at him beneath lowered lashes as she shook her head. "No, you gave me the cure."

His laughter was throaty and deep as he swept her into his arms, holding her against his bare chest. "Let's see how thoroughly cured you are, woman." He leaned forward to kiss her while he carried her to the rug in front of the roaring fire.

THE EDITOR'S CORNER

It seems only a breathless moment ago that we launched LOVESWEPT into the crowded sea of romance publishing. And yet with publication of this month's titles we mark the end of LOVESWEPT'S first full year on the stands. An anniversary is a wonderful thing for many reasons . . . and not the least of them is that it prompts a little reflection about the past twelve months and the twelve months to come. As you know, we run a statement about our publishing goals for the LOVESWEPT romances in the front of each of our novels. Reviewing our books for the past year, I can't help feeling proud of the numbers of times we were able to reach the goal of providing you with a "keeper." Heartfelt bravos and gratitude to our wonderful authors and to the scores of people on the Bantam Books staff who've made this possible. Each time we've reached the goal of providing a truly fresh, creative love story, we find that our goal expands and we have a new standard of freshness and creativity to strive for. And, so, we've grown professionally and personally and will go on growing.

Each title for next month represents to us one of the overall ingredients we want in the books in our line. **TO SEE THE DAISIES . . . FIRST** symbolizes the freshness and optimism of our romances; **NO RED ROSES,** again a flower image, represents the kind of true romance of our stories; **THAT OLD FEELING,** certainly expresses our goal of providing novels that truly touch the emotions, that can sometimes make you laugh—and sometimes make you cry; and **SOME-THING DIFFERENT . . .** is the phrase that describes the highest of our goals—and the hardest to reach—to

(continued)

bring you very creative love stories full of delightful surprises. But, I bet you want me to move away from all the general talk and settle down into the specific— namely, letting you know about the four stories you have to look forward to next month.

In **TO SEE THE DAISIES . . . FIRST,** LOVESWEPT #43, Billie Green gives us another of her captivating love stories full of humor and tinged with pathos. Ben Garrison knew his life was lacking something, but he didn't know what until he met an enchanting woman who wore only a man's trenchcoat and had absolutely no idea who she was! Ben named her Sunny, because she was as life-giving as the sun's warm rays. He opened his home and his heart to her, but soon her past threatened both her and their love.

Ah, now you'll know! Mike Novacek isn't the hero of **NO RED ROSES,** as you probably realized from that broad hint we gave you in last month's Editor's Corner. Rex Brody is the hero and what an irresistible one! Iris really knows how to give us a lovable man, doesn't she? In **NO RED ROSES,** LOVESWEPT #44, heroine Tamara Ledford should have been prepared for almost anything because she'd grown up with her psychic aunt. But even her aunt couldn't fully warn her about Rex, and how the famous singer would whirl into her life and whisk her away. Tamara allowed herself to fall in love with Rex as he showered her with flowers that symbolized beauty and sensuality while she hid her hurt that he never gave her red roses, the flowers that mean love. Thanks to Iris for giving that wonderful, charming Rex the love he so richly deserved.

Remember Fayrene Preston's first LOVESWEPT #4, **SILVER MIRACLES?** From line one you could just feel that hot, sultry Texas night surrounding her characters. Here again in **THAT OLD FEELING,** LOVESWEPT #45, Fayrene is at her most sensually evocative, bringing settings and senses to full life.

Christopher Saxon wants his wife Lisa back, and follows her on vacation to Baja, California, where he convinces her that they should try again. But even as Lisa is melting in his embrace, she is worrying: for, if their love has survived their separation, have the problems that drove them apart years earlier survived, too?

Kay Hooper's LOVESWEPT #46, **SOMETHING DIFFERENT**, delivers just what the title says it will. Kay's superb originality and wit has never been shown off better than in this love story which is a delicious brew of delectable characters, both human and animal. The heroine, Gypsy Taylor, is a famous mystery writer who doesn't believe heroes exist in the modern-day world. Chase Mitchell sets out to prove her wrong. He gives her the Lone Ranger, Zorro—and himself. Some of Chase's antics are outrageous, almost as outrageous as Gypsy's piratical cat named Corsair!

As we celebrate our first year, our warmest thoughts go out to each and every loyal reader who has taken our LOVESWEPT romances off the shelves and into her heart. Cards and letters from fans along with the generous support of booksellers have made this a year full of beautiful memories. As we promised the day we started LOVESWEPT and have promised every day since—we will always try to publish love stories you'll never forget by authors you'll always remember.

Sincerely,

Carolyn Nichols

Carolyn Nichols
   Editor
LOVESWEPT
Bantam Books, Inc.
666 Fifth Avenue
New York, NY 10103

LOVESWEPT

Love Stories you'll never forget by authors you'll always remember

☐	21603	**Heaven's Price #1** Sandra Brown	$1.95
☐	21604	**Surrender #2** Helen Mittermeyer	$1.95
☐	21600	**The Joining Stone #3** Noelle Berry McCue	$1.95
☐	21601	**Silver Miracles #4** Fayrene Preston	$1.95
☐	21605	**Matching Wits #5** Carla Neggers	$1.95
☐	21606	**A Love for All Time #6** Dorothy Garlock	$1.95
☐	21607	**A Tryst With Mr. Lincoln? #7** Billie Green	$1.95
☐	21602	**Temptation's Sting #8** Helen Conrad	$1.95
☐	21608	**December 32nd . . . And Always #9** Marie Michael	$1.95
☐	21609	**Hard Drivin' Man #10** Nancy Carlson	$1.95
☐	21610	**Beloved Intruder #11** Noelle Berry McCue	$1.95
☐	21611	**Hunter's Payne #12** Joan J. Domning	$1.95
☐	21618	**Tiger Lady #13** Joan Domning	$1.95
☐	21613	**Stormy Vows #14** Iris Johansen	$1.95
☐	21614	**Brief Delight #15** Helen Mittermeyer	$1.95
☐	21616	**A Very Reluctant Knight #16** Billie Green	$1.95
☐	21617	**Tempest at Sea #17** Iris Johansen	$1.95
☐	21619	**Autumn Flames #18** Sara Orwig	$1.95
☐	21620	**Pfarr Lake Affair #19** Joan Domning	$1.95
☐	21621	**Heart on a String #20** Carla Neggars	$1.95
☐	21622	**The Seduction of Jason #21** Fayrene Preston	$1.95
☐	21623	**Breakfast In Bed #22** Sandra Brown	$1.95
☐	21624	**Taking Savannah #23** Becky Combs	$1.95
☐	21625	**The Reluctant Lark #24** Iris Johansen	$1.95

Prices and availability subject to change without notice.

Buy them at your local bookstore or use this handy coupon for ordering:

Bantam Books, Inc., Dept. SW, 414 East Golf Road, Des Plaines, Ill. 60016

Please send me the books I have checked above. I am enclosing $_____ (please add $1.25 to cover postage and handling). Send check or money order—no cash or C.O.D.'s please.

Mr/Ms_____

Address _____

City/State_____ Zip_____

SW—3/84

Please allow four to six weeks for delivery. This offer expires 9/84.

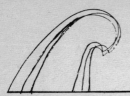

LOVESWEPT

Love Stories you'll never forget by authors you'll always remember

☐	21630	LIGHTNING THAT LINGERS #25	$1.95
		Sharon & Tom Curtis	
☐	21631	ONCE IN A BLUE MOON #26 Millie J. Green	$1.95
☐	21632	THE BRONZED HAWK #27 Iris Johansen	$1.95
☐	21637	LOVE, CATCH A WILD BIRD #28 Anne Reisser	$1.95
☐	21626	THE LADY AND THE UNICORN #29	$1.95
		Iris Johansen	
☐	21628	WINNER TAKE ALL #30 Nancy Holder	$1.95
☐	21635	THE GOLDEN VALKYRIE #31 Iris Johansen	$1.95
☐	21638	C.J.'s FATE #32 Kay Hooper	$1.95
☐	21639	THE PLANTING SEASON #33 Dorothy Garlock	$1.95
☐	21629	FOR LOVE OF SAMI #34 Fayrene Preston	$1.95
☐	21627	THE TRUSTWORTHY REDHEAD #35 Iris Johansen	$1.95
☐	21636	A TOUCH OF MAGIC #36 Carla Neggers	$1.95
☐	21641	IRRESISTIBLE FORCES #37 Marie Michael	$1.95
☐	21642	TEMPORARY ANGEL #38 Billie Green	$1.95
☐	21646	KIRSTEN'S INHERITANCE #39 Joan Domning	$1.95
☐	21645	RETURN TO SANTA FLORES #40 Iris Johansen	$1.95
☐	21656	THE SOPHISTICATED MOUNTAIN GAL #41	$1.95
		Joan Bramsch	
☐	21655	HEAT WAVE #42 Sara Orwig	$1.95

Prices and availability subject to change without notice.

Buy them at your local bookstore or use this handy coupon for ordering:

Bantam Books, Inc., Dept. SW, 414 East Golf Road, Des Plaines, Ill. 60016

Please send me the books I have checked above. I am enclosing $_____
(please add $1.25 to cover postage and handling). Send check or money order
—no cash or C.O.D.'s please.

Mr/Mrs/Miss _____

Address_____

City_____ State/Zip_____

SW2—4/84

Please allow four to six weeks for delivery. This offer expires 10/84.